Welcome

The 1984 film *Amadeus* may have played fast and loose with the facts (for starters, Salieri didn't poison Mozart, and he most certainly had no hand in completing the Requiem), but an early scene in the film is striking for the extraordinarily poignant way it tackles the subject of Mozart's genius.

Salieri, confined to a lunatic asylum having admitted to killing his fellow composer, describes to a visiting doctor his first encounter with Mozart's *Serenade for Winds*, K361: 'On the page, it looked nothing. The beginning simple, almost comic. Just a pulse: bassoons, basset horns, like a rusty squeeze box. And then suddenly, high above it, an oboe. A single note hanging there unwavering... This was a music I'd never heard... It seemed to me that I was hearing the voice of God.' It's a breathtaking description that gets close to explaining the essence of Mozart's art of moulding complex ideas into seemingly simple, effortless works of astonishing timeless beauty.

Since his death in 1791, Mozart's music has remained popular, his life has become the subject of a great deal of scrutiny and his legacy is continually debated. Over the years, *BBC Music Magazine* has explored many facets of Mozart's life and music – so we thought it high time we assembled the very best from the past 20 years for this exclusive guide. I do hope it will give you a fresh perspective on this most brilliant of musical talents and help you continue to discover his wonderful music.

Oliver Condy *Editor*

Credits

EDITORIAL
Editor **Oliver Condy**
Deputy Editor **Jeremy Pound**
Editor-in-chief **Paul McGuinness**
Production Editor **Mel Woodward**
Subeditor **Rebecca Candler**
Editorial Assistant **Emma Jolliffe**

ART & PICTURES
Art Editor **Sheu-Kuei Ho**
Designer **Lisa White**
Picture Editor **James Cutmore**
Picture Researcher
Rhiannon Furbear-Williams

PRESS AND PUBLIC RELATIONS
Press Officer **Carolyn Wray**
0117 314 8812
carolyn.wray@immediate.co.uk

CIRCULATION / ADVERTISING
Circulation Manager **Rob Brock**
Advertising Director **Caroline Herbert**
Senior Advertising Manager **Tom Drew**

PRODUCTION
Production Director **Sarah Powell**
Production Manager **Emma McGuinness**
Reprographics **Tony Hunt and Chris Sutch**

PUBLISHING
Publisher **Andrew Davies**
Publishing Director **Andy Healy**
Managing Director **Andy Marshall**
Chairman **Stephen Alexander**
Deputy Chairman **Peter Phippen**
CEO **Tom Bureau**

WORDS: Rob Ainsley, Terry Barfoot, Gavin Dixon, Misha Donat, Cliff Eisen, Hilary Finch, Anthony Holden, Martin Hoyle, Erik Levi, Fiona Maddocks, Jeremy Pound, Chris de Souza, HC Robbins Landon, Neal Zaslaw

Front Cover: **Superstock**

CONTENTS

Mozart: A life

From working for the Archbishop of Salzburg to writing acclaimed operas in Vienna, Mozart's life was full of ups and downs but his legacy lives on

Mozart becomes Archbishop **Colloredo's** concertmaster.

In Italy, Mozart writes choruses and arias for *Lucio Silla*.

Back in Salzburg, Mozart writes three vocal works: *Apollo et Hyacinthus*, the first part of *Die Schuldigkeit des ersten Gebots* and the *Grabmusik*.

At just five years old, **Mozart composes a miniature** *Andante* and *Allegro*. Leopold arranges concerts to showcase his talent.

In October, Mozart is **appointed honorary concertmaster** at the Salzburg court.

Mozart turns away from court and church pieces to focus on instrumental and secular vocal music.

La finta semplice is **performed** at court in May.

1772

1761

1765

1769

1775

1755

1763

1773

1775

The Mozart family sets out on its first **tour of Europe**, travelling through the major cities of Germany, France, The Netherlands, England, Switzerland and Belgium.

Mozart is denied an opera commission for *La finta semplice*.

The Mozart family moves to a larger apartment, reflecting Leopold's view of their rising status in Salzburg society.

1756

1768

1770

Wolfgang Amadeus Mozart is **born on 27 January** in Salzburg, Austria.

Leopold Mozart accuses theatre director Giuseppe Afflisio of conspiring against him by claiming that he ghostwrote Wolfgang's music.

Mozart is commissioned to write an opera, *Mitridate, re di Ponto*, for the carnival season in Milan.

On 5 July, Pope Clemens XIV makes Mozart a **Knight of the Golden Spur**.

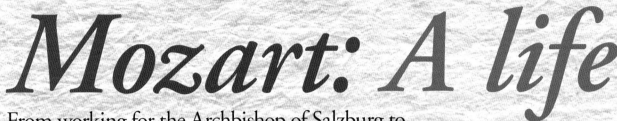

FAMILY MOMENT: Mozart and his sister Nannerl perform a duet

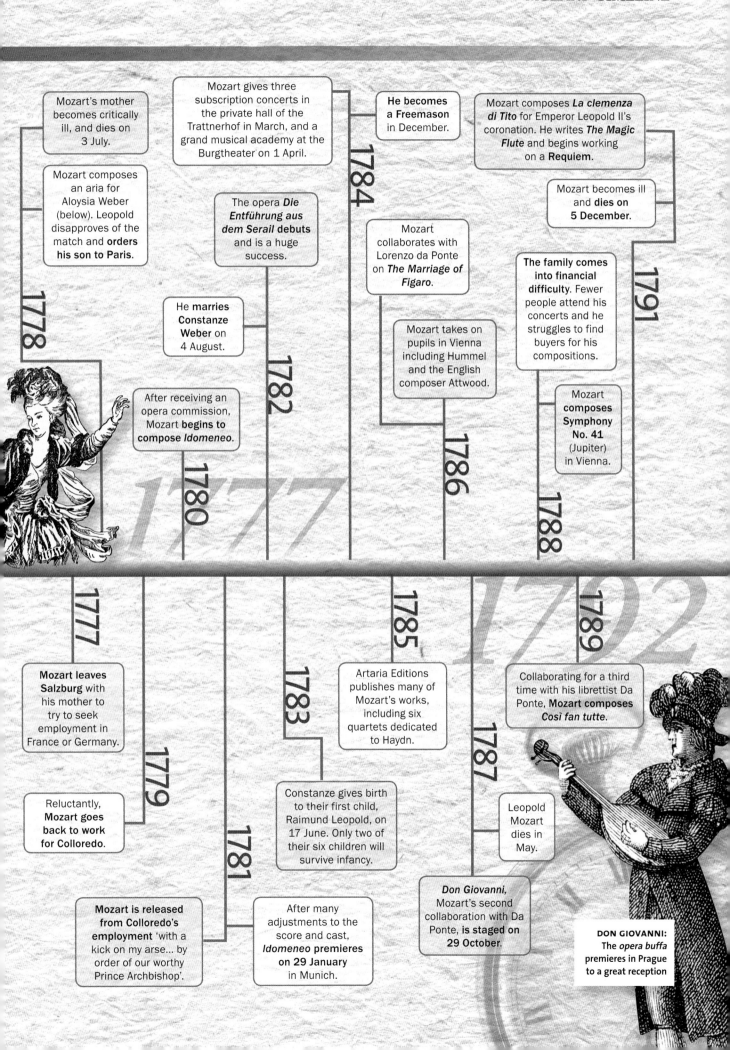

Mozart's mother becomes critically ill, and dies on 3 July.

Mozart composes an aria for Aloysia Weber (below). Leopold disapproves of the match and **orders his son to Paris**.

1778

Mozart gives three subscription concerts in the private hall of the Trattnerhof in March, and a grand musical academy at the Burgtheater on 1 April.

1784

He becomes a Freemason in December.

The opera *Die Entführung aus dem Serail* debuts and is a huge success.

Mozart composes *La clemenza di Tito* for Emperor Leopold II's coronation. He writes *The Magic Flute* and begins working on a **Requiem**.

1791

Mozart becomes ill and **dies on 5 December**.

Mozart collaborates with Lorenzo da Ponte on *The Marriage of Figaro*.

The family comes into financial difficulty. Fewer people attend his concerts and he struggles to find buyers for his compositions.

He **marries Constanze Weber** on 4 August.

1782

Mozart takes on pupils in Vienna including Hummel and the English composer Attwood.

1786

Mozart composes Symphony No. 41 (Jupiter) in Vienna.

After receiving an opera commission, Mozart **begins to compose *Idomeneo***.

1780

1777

1788

1777

1792

1789

Mozart leaves Salzburg with his mother to try to seek employment in France or Germany.

1783

Artaria Editions publishes many of Mozart's works, including six quartets dedicated to Haydn.

1785

Collaborating for a third time with his librettist Da Ponte, **Mozart composes *Così fan tutte***.

1779

Reluctantly, **Mozart goes back to work for Colloredo**.

Constanze gives birth to their first child, Raimund Leopold, on 17 June. Only two of their six children will survive infancy.

1787

Leopold Mozart dies in May.

1781

Mozart is released from Colloredo's employment 'with a kick on my arse... by order of our worthy Prince Archbishop'.

After many adjustments to the score and cast, *Idomeneo* premieres on 29 January in Munich.

Don Giovanni, Mozart's second collaboration with Da Ponte, is staged on 29 October.

DON GIOVANNI: The *opera buffa* premieres in Prague to a great reception

MOZART

MODERN PERFORMANCES

DON GIOVANNI

Salzburg Festival, 2008. Dir. Claus Guth

Murder, seduction, deception and revenge – *Don Giovanni* has it all. The opera was Mozart's second collaboration with librettist Lorenzo Da Ponte.

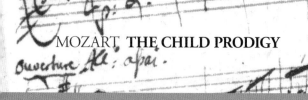

THE CHILD PRODIGY

Mozart was a gifted pianist from an extremely young age and his family was quick to capitalise on the young boy's talents

Of the seven children born to the Salzburg court musician, Leopold Mozart, and his wife Anna Maria, only two survived infancy. Maria Anna, known as Nannerl, was born in 1751; five years later, the seventh child, Wolfgang Amadeus, was born on 27 January 1756.

Both children soon proved that they had prodigious gifts in music, especially Wolfgang. At the age of only three, he could sit at the keyboard, and delight in the sounds he produced. By the time of the boy's fourth birthday, his father was able to teach him simple pieces, as his sister later recalled: 'He learned a sonata in an hour, and a minuet in half an hour, so that he could play it faultlessly and with the greatest delicacy, and keeping exactly in time. He made such progress that by the age of five he was already composing little pieces of his own.'

This precocious talent excited Leopold so much that he determined to change his own priorities in order to maximise his son's musical potential, and to make an internationally famous musician of him. He therefore made his own career at the Salzburg court a secondary consideration, though in this his motives were far from pure. For he recognised that his son's virtuosity made him an extraordinary phenomenon, which he hoped would prove an attractive and financially rewarding proposition at other, more prestigious centres across Europe.

Thus it was that Leopold and his two children set out from Salzburg in January 1762, just days before Wolfgang's sixth birthday. They stayed for three weeks at ▶

> At the age of only three, Mozart could sit at the keyboard, and delight in the sounds he produced

ALAMY

A ROYAL TREAT:
Mozart first performed for the Austrian court when he was just six years old

generous, and one performance led to others by recommendation. It was in November 1763 that they arrived at Paris, a city whose size was daunting in comparison with provincial Salzburg. A performance before the King, Louis XV, was arranged for New Year's Day, and Nannerl noted in her diary that her brother 'played the organ in the court chapel, before the entire court, and won the applause of all'. There were many invitations from the Parisian nobility, affording Wolfgang the opportunity to show his expertise as a violinist as well as a keyboard player.

A musical education

The reception they received in Paris encouraged the Mozarts to proceed to London, and they crossed the channel from Calais to Dover on 22 April 1764. It was while Leopold was suffering from a severe throat infection that Wolfgang turned his attention towards composition. The London public, as well as King George III and Queen Charlotte, readily took to the Mozarts, and their performances were very popular.

At the same time as making his fame and his family's fortune, Mozart was gaining a musical education the like of which no composer before or since has encountered. The famous castrato (male soprano) Giovanni Manzuoli observed that the boy's talents were purely instrumental, and volunteered to teach him the art of singing. More important, however, was the time he spent with two German musicians who were based in London: Karl Friedrich

the Munich court, where they performed for Maximilian Joseph, Elector of Bavaria. Later in the year, now accompanied by the children's mother, they journeyed to Vienna where they were received at the Schönbrunn Palace. There they performed to the acclaim of the family of the Empress Maria Theresa, and the audience included the seven-year-old princess Marie Antoinette, later to be Queen of France. She, it seems, particularly enjoyed the performance and it is rumoured that Mozart proposed to her afterwards!

Thanks to Leopold's cunning management, these first trips proved so successful that, just six months after returning to Salzburg, he led the family on another tour, which would last for more than three years. The destinations included London and Paris, but the itinerary

was necessarily flexible, since Leopold could not be sure of the presence of the influential nobility at any particular time. There were visits to many large cities, including Munich, Augsburg, Stuttgart, Frankfurt, Koblenz and Cologne in Germany, as well as Liège and Brussels in Belgium, then part of the Netherlands. At Frankfurt, the audience included a 14-year-old Johann Wolfgang von Goethe, a future German writer, artist and politician. Johann later recalled 'the impression made by the little man with his wig and sword'.

The pattern was soon established. Although there were no payments as such, the gifts the Mozarts received were

IN TUNE: Created by Louis-Ernest Barrias, this marble statue depicts Mozart tuning his violin

Abel and Johann Christian Bach. Mozart became Bach's composition pupil, making arrangements of several pieces and absorbing the older man's style.

The Mozarts stayed in London for several months, but their later concerts proved somewhat less remunerative; the novelty of the wunderkind was wearing off. Following the suggestion of the Dutch ambassador, they made their way to The Hague and Amsterdam, where they stayed

> Mozart gained a musical education the like of which no composer before or since has encountered

for seven months. The duration of this stay was partly because both Nannerl and Wolfgang contracted typhus and nearly died. The homeward journey included a visit to Brussels and another to Paris, before several stops in Switzerland and a last visit to Munich. At last, on 30 November 1766, they reached Salzburg. Brother and sister were growing up; Nannerl was now a girl of 15, Wolfgang a ten-year-old whose behaviour, according to those who met him, was remarkably unspoiled by his exploits and experiences.

The composer is born

The grand tour provided Mozart with a substantial musical education, and in those three and a half years he certainly learned a great deal more than he would have done by remaining in Salzburg. Not only had his stylistic awareness grown rapidly, his performing technique had, of necessity, been tested to the full. The opportunity to compose his first work for the stage soon followed. This was *Apollo et Hyacinthus*, an intermezzo designed to be performed between the acts of a Latin play at Salzburg University. And his first opera was not long delayed; *La finta semplice*, completed in July 1768, resulted from a Viennese commission by the Emperor Joseph II. It finally reached the stage after a series of intrigues involving other opera composers. Without doubt, Mozart the composer, at the age of 12, was being taken seriously. And the advance of the young composer was certainly Leopold's priority from now on, for he viewed it as a duty to God, 'to prove the miracle to the world'. *Terry Barfoot* ∎

LEOPOLD MOZART

*Born Augsburg, 14 November 1719
Died Salzburg, 28 May 1787*

MOZART'S FATHER, Leopold, was the son of an Augsburg bookbinder. His family supported him through a broad education in which his musical studies revealed his diverse talents: as an organist, violinist and singer. However, the family viewed this education as the basis for entry into the priesthood, to which end Leopold entered the Benedictine University of Salzburg. He enjoyed academic success but he did not complete the course, his commitment to music taking priority over other options.

At the age of just 24, Leopold became a violinist in the court ensemble of Archbishop Schrattenbach, rising to Vice-Kapellmeister in 1763. His reputation spread across Europe when he published his *Versuch einer gründlichen Violinschule*, the first important book on the techniques and styles of violin playing, which was translated in several languages. This was in 1756, the year in which his son, Wolfgang Amadeus, was born. To this day the book remains the most important source of reference for 18th century performing styles.

Leopold was a talented composer, but he gave up both his creative work and his career as a violinist when he realised that his children were especially gifted. He decided to devote himself to their artistic cause, acting as teacher and private secretary, valet and impresario, propagandist and travel agent. These priorities undoubtedly restricted his career and, following the death of his wife in 1778, he became increasingly frustrated at his lack of influence over Wolfgang, who sought his independence as man and musician.

When Leopold died, the Abbot of St Peter's in Salzburg, Domenicus Hagenauer, wrote in his diary: 'Leopold Mozart was a man of much wit and wisdom. He spent most of his days in court service, yet had the misfortune always to be persecuted and was far less beloved here than in other great places of Europe. He reached an age of 68 years.'

HOME TOWN: The population of Salzburg in the 18th century was around 16,000

AN ARTIST'S PERSPECTIVE: AFH Naumann's impression of Salzburg towards the end of the 18th century when Mozart, Haydn and Salieri would have lived there

SALZBURG
& BEYOND

Mozart's reputation was well established and everyone wanted the talented musician to perform for them. From 1772 to 1779 he travelled extensively, expanding his repertoire and, for the first time, experiencing freedom

From the first, opera proved a huge attraction to Mozart, and since Italy was the centre of the operatic world, the country's lure was magnetic. So it was that in December 1769, father and son set out for Milan, where they were most warmly received and an opera was commissioned for the next season. The Italian journey proved lengthy enough to allow the composition of this opera. *Mitridate, Rè di Ponto*, K87, was introduced to great acclaim, with Mozart directing the performance from the keyboard.

At Bologna, the eminent composer and theorist Padre Martini was impressed by Mozart's expertise; at Florence, Wolfgang was befriended by Thomas Linley, a gifted English musician of his own age; and at Rome the honours could hardly have been greater, as Pope Clement XIV conferred upon him the highest class of the Order of the Golden Spur, accorded to only one musician previously, Orlando di Lasso. In March 1771, the Mozarts were back in Salzburg, but the following August they

were en route for Italy once again, having received a lucrative commission from Milan. The serenata *Ascanio in Alba*, K111, was performed that October after the wedding of Archduke Ferdinand, Governor of Lombardy, to Princess Beatrice of Modena. Mozart's letter to his sister gives an indication of his creative facility, since

---

Pope Clement XIV awarded Mozart the Order of the Golden Spur

---

he was able to compose in less-than-ideal conditions: 'Upstairs we have a violinist, downstairs another one, in the next room a singing master who gives lessons, and in the other room opposite ours an oboist. That is good fun when you are composing. It gives you plenty of ideas.' After hearing

Mozart's music that autumn, the opera composer Johann Hasse observed: 'This boy will consign us all to oblivion.'

European travels
A third Italian journey was undertaken in November 1772, for the production of the *opera seria Lucio Silla*, K135, which had been commissioned as the result of the popularity of *Ascanio in Alba*. The music was given a certain formality, in keeping with the noble characters who feature in the drama, and Mozart conceived it with particular singers in mind. Most notable among these was the eminent castrato Venanzio Rauzzini, for whom he also composed a showpiece motet, *Exsultate jubilate*, K165.

Instrumental music played an important part in Mozart's development during these years as well. The first six string quartets were products of the third Italian journey, and after the return to Salzburg there came a wealth of fine compositions. These reveal that, in his teenage years, Mozart's original and creative genius was now ▶

TYPES OF OPERA IN THE 18TH CENTURY

IDOMENEO: Performed in March 2003 at the Deutsche Oper Berlin, Germany

During Mozart's lifetime, opera was the most popular evening entertainment in all the major European cities

OPERA SERIA

Opera seria was the main operatic genre of the early and mid-18th century, and was going out of fashion during Mozart's lifetime. However, it remained important, particularly when operas were commissioned in connection with formal state occasions. (Both *Idomeneo* and *La clemenza di Tito* resulted from commissions such as these.)

The subject matter was intended to be of noble outlook, based on stories from ancient Greece or Rome, while the musical style was founded upon the requirements for virtuoso display of star singers, including castrati. The dramatic structure centred upon sequences of arias, numbers that were linked by recitatives (half spoken, half sung, with keyboard or orchestral accompaniment), while the language of performance was Italian, the international language of opera.

OPERA BUFFA

The principal influence on the early development of *opera buffa* was the *commedia dell'arte*, whose influence spread from Italy all over Europe. Characters were drawn from real life, thus offering a contrast from *opera seria*. In due course, for instance in the later works of Mozart, such as *The Marriage of Figaro* and *Così fan tutte*, the comic element became only one aspect of the *buffo* style, and it was perfectly possible to develop a range of characterisation which was sensitive to the realistic portrayal of ordinary people and their emotions.

The Countess in Mozart's *Figaro*, who is saddened by the infidelities of her husband, is an excellent example. By the time Mozart settled in Vienna, *opera buffa* had replaced *opera seria* as the central operatic genre. Performances were given in Italian and the dramatic structure remained that of number opera, with musical scenes linked by recitatives. While arias remained central to the scheme, ensembles became increasingly important, because of the possibilities they offered for developing the relationships between the characters.

SINGSPIEL

Singspiel is a German music drama, or opera, in which the musical numbers are separated by spoken dialogue. Its French equivalent is the opéra-comique, its English the ballad opera. Mozart composed various works in this genre, of which the finest are *Die Entführung aus dem Serail* and *Die Zauberflöte*.

The *Singspiel* tradition of the 18th century was focused upon sentimentality, light comedy and folk ingredients. However, from the 1780s, not least in Vienna, the melodic style became increasingly bravura and the plots introduced magical, supernatural elements, and aspects of comic farce not unlike those found in the English pantomime. As in his treatments of the other operatic genres, Mozart transcended the limitations imposed by this formula, particularly in *Die Zauberflöte*, where a deeply serious approach exists alongside that of the conventional comedy.

flowering. Many mass settings, divertimenti and serenades were written for the court and various local families, and these 'entertainment' pieces, conceived for the amusement of the aristocracy at dinner, have a special charm and fluency that have proved of lasting value.

Perhaps it is in the orchestral music of the mid-1770s that Mozart's new stature can most clearly be recognised. The series of violin concertos, written for either Mozart himself or the assistant orchestral leader Antonio Brunetti, are superbly crafted and gloriously lyrical, but it is through the symphonies that the young composer's progress can most clearly be shown. Whereas the earlier examples were short pieces in the style of older composers and on the scale of operatic overtures, several of the symphonies of these years are highly individual and subtle. Particularly fine are the stormy G minor Symphony No. 25, K183, and the elegant A major Symphony No. 29, K201, whose contrasting personalities confirm the wide expressive range of which Mozart was now capable.

> 'Off with you to Paris! And that soon! Find your place among great people' Leopold Mozart

---

The most substantial of the 'entertainment' works is the *Haffner Serenade*, K250, written for a family wedding celebration and containing a violin concerto within its seven movements.

Piano concertos

In January 1777, inspired by the visiting French virtuoso Victoire Jenamy, Mozart composed his finest concerto to date – the Piano Concerto No.9 in E flat, K271. Until 2004, the piece was known as the *Jeunehomme* Concerto, as there was much confusion over who Mozart had written it for. In this concerto, Mozart was possibly laying the plans for his own visit to Paris, on which he would set out later that year. At any rate, he composed a concerto on a more extended scale than he ever had previously. This concerto raises the genre to a new level of distinction and indicates the qualities he would consistently achieve in his great Viennese concertos.

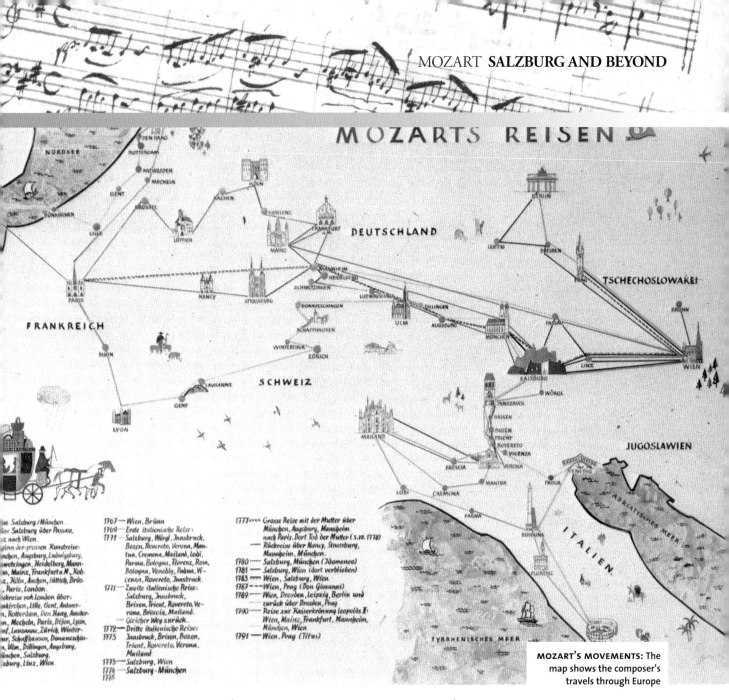

MOZART'S MOVEMENTS: The map shows the composer's travels through Europe

The orchestral music of this period is written for the standard Salzburg ensemble, comprising pairs of horns, oboes and strings. Yet for all his achievements in his native city, Mozart's travels had made him aware of its artistic limitations. And there were now other problems besides. In December 1771, Prince-Archbishop Sigismund von Schrattenbach died, and was succeeded by Hieronymous Joseph von Paula, Count of Colloredo. Among the new Archbishop's first actions was to grant the Mozarts leave of absence for their third Italian journey, but his countenance would be less benign than his predecessor's: his policy was to govern punctiliously and exact like service from his employees. Leopold was his Vice-Kapellmeister and Wolfgang his Konzertmeister (orchestral leader), and he had high expectations of them.

Frustrated by the limitations of Salzburg, the Mozarts planned another extended tour, this time to Paris, but Colloredo

made it clear that he would not tolerate such a venture. He explained that he did not intend to allow his servants 'to go running around like beggars', and he made his position crystal clear: 'Father and son, in accordance with the gospel, have permission to seek their fortune elsewhere.' In other words, if they left they would be leaving for good. Therefore Leopold remained at home when Wolfgang set off in August 1777, accompanied by his mother. The journey was organised in a manner that recalled the earlier 'Grand Tour', since it was financed by the fees and gifts received for performances en route. The search for a prestigious appointment was also a keen priority.

At Munich, the Elector Bavaria was full of praise for the performance he heard, but his court had no need of another musician. At Mannheim, Mozart delighted not only in the quality of the splendid orchestra but in the company of the Weber family,

with whom he stayed. He fell in love with Aloysia, the second of the four daughters, and even suggested changing his plans to accompany her on a trip to Italy. However, he continued on his way to Paris, Leopold's letter insisting upon it: 'Off with you to Paris! And that soon! Find your place among great people.'

The return to Salzburg

In Paris, Mozart's experiences proved frustrating, and the hoped-for opportunities did not materialise, though he did write the magnificent Symphony No 31, K297. Any musical affairs were soon overshadowed by the death of his mother in July, following a short illness. He returned home, meeting again in Munich with the Weber family, who had moved there from Mannheim; however, Aloysia now showed no interest in him. He finally reached Salzburg in January 1779, and rejoined the service of the Archbishop. *Terry Barfoot* ■

THE BOSS: Mozart and the Archbishop of Salzburg, Count Colloredo had a turbulent relationship

GETTY

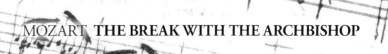

THE BREAK WITH THE ARCHBISHOP

He had been under his employment since 1771, but an increasingly strained relationship with the Archbishop of Salzburg was about to end as Mozart lost his position and became a freelance composer in Vienna

Leopold persuaded Archbishop Colloredo to take Wolfgang back into his service, and he was installed not only in his previous position as Konzertmeister, but also as court organist, with a generous salary. Perhaps this was recognition of his growing reputation; perhaps it was simply the contingency of filling positions that had become vacant. Mozart's duties included performing music in church, at court and in the chapel, giving instruction to the choirboys, and composing church and secular music as required.

Mozart returned to employment and life in Salzburg for the sake of his father, rather than to fulfil his own wishes. In doing so, he felt he was 'committing the greatest folly in the world'. Leopold had suggested that the Paris trip had been intended as a means of obtaining 'a good court appointment, or, if this should fail, to go off to some big city where large sums of money can be earned'. The trip achieved neither of these aims. Moreover, it extended Mozart's emotional experience in three significant ways: through the death of his mother; the unhappy love affair with Aloysia Weber; and a period of freedom from his father's controlling influence.

> Mozart returned to life in Salzburg for the sake of his father, rather than to fulfil his own wishes

Before Mozart left Paris, he responded to Leopold's urgent pleas for him to return home: 'When I read [your letter], I trembled with joy, for I fancied myself already in your arms. It is true – and you will confess this yourself – that no great fortune is awaiting me in Salzburg. Yet when I think of once more embracing you and my dear sister with all my heart, I care for no other advantage. To tell you my real feelings, the only thing that disgusts me about Salzburg is the impossibility of mixing freely with the people and the low estimation in which the musicians are held there; and that the Archbishop has no confidence in the experiences of intelligent people, who have seen the world... If the Archbishop would only trust me, I should soon make his orchestra famous; of this there can be no doubt... Dear Father! I must confess that were it not for the pleasure of seeing you both again, I really could not decide to accept.'

New compositions

Mozart's recent music had included two flute concertos – the second adapted from an oboe concerto – and three flute quartets, all written for a wealthy Dutch amateur, De Jean, who resided at Mannheim, Germany. He also composed the Concerto for Flute and Harp, K299, commissioned in Paris ▶

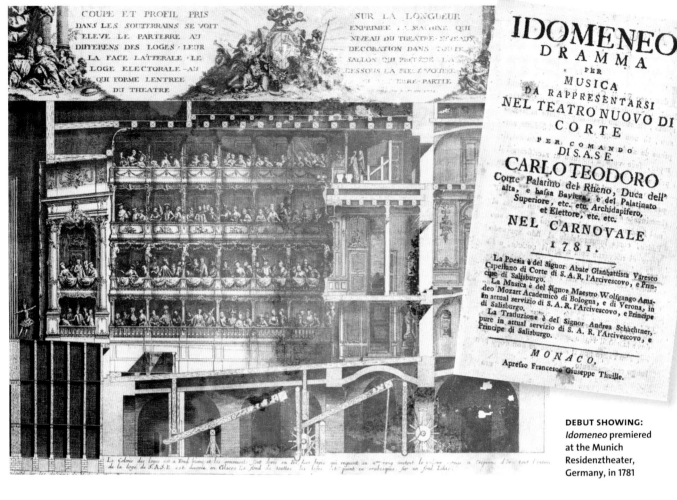

IDOMENEO
DRAMMA
PER
MUSICA
DA RAPPRESENTARSI
NEL TEATRO NUOVO DI
CORTE
PER COMANDO
DI S.A.S.E.
CARLO TEODORO
Conte Palatino del Rheno, Duca dell'
alta, e bassa Baviera, e del Palatinato
Superiore, etc. etc. Archidapifero,
et Elettore, etc. etc.
NEL CARNOVALE
1781.

La Poesia è del Signor Abate Gianbattista Varesco
Capellano di Corte di S. A. R. l'Arcivescovo, e Principe di Salisburgo.
La Musica è del Signor Maestro Wolfgango Ama-
deo Mozart Academico di Bologna, e di Verona, in
in attual servizio di S. A. R. l'Arcivescovo, e Principe
di Salisburgo.
La Traduzione è del Signor Andrea Schächtner,
pure in attual servizio di S. A. R. l'Arcivescovo, e
Principe di Salisburgo.

MONACO,
Appresso Francesco Giuseppe Thuille.

DEBUT SHOWING:
Idomeneo premiered
at the Munich
Residenztheater,
Germany, in 1781

by the Duc de Guines and his daughter, and a new type of composition he had encountered at Mannheim, which he wrote for the Concert spirituel: the Sinfonia Concertante, K297b, for wind instruments and orchestra. He also dedicated a set of six Violin Sonatas, K301-6, to Maria Elisabeth, wife of the Mannheim Elector.

In Salzburg, Mozart continued to compose according to opportunity. Among the first new works was the splendid *Coronation Mass*, K317, so called because of the anniversary, on the fifth Sunday after Whitsun, of the miraculous image of the Virgin at a nearby church. Two Vesper settings, the *Vesperae de Domenica*, K321, and the *Vesperae solennes de confessore*, K339, date from 1780, and show a more personal response to the possibilities offered by church music than Mozart had found hitherto.

The finest of the orchestral works of the period is certainly the Sinfonia Concertante, K364, for violin and viola, another example of the Mannheim influence, but which transcends its models by Christian Cannabich and Carl Stamitz. There were two

more symphonies: the light and charming Symphony No. 33 in B flat, K319, is scored for the usual Salzburg ensemble of strings with oboes, bassoons and horns; but the Symphony No. 34 in C major, K338, continues the style of the earlier Paris Symphony, since it is a grand affair with trumpets and drums. The 1770s also brought a new interest in solo keyboard music; the sonatas of this period have an enduring value and a wide expressive range: K310 in A minor, for example, is his first minor-key sonata, and is a bold response to the new fashion of the time, with its fiery emotional commitment: the *Sturm und Drang* (Storm and Stress).

One of the chief frustrations of musical life in Salzburg was the lack of opportunity in music for the stage. The small theatre there was used mainly for German plays and entertainments given by touring companies, and Mozart certainly frequented it. For this theatre he composed a small-scale *Singspiel, Zaide*, K344, which anticipates the style of his first Viennese opera, *Die Entführung aus dem Serail*. There was also the splendid incidental music, K345, for a

production of *Thamos, König von Aegypten*, a play by an acquaintance of Mozart's, Tobias von Gebler. But these were small-scale exceptions to the rule – in order to compose operas, Mozart would have to look elsewhere.

Writing an opera
The opportunity soon arrived, in the form of a commission for a full-scale *opera seria* from the Bavarian court at Munich. The circumstances were particularly favourable, as it suited Colloredo's purpose to have his court musician given a prestigious creative responsibility by a larger and more powerful neighbour.

STARRING ROLE:
Anton Raaf in his
leading role of
King Idomeneo

VIENNESE AUDIENCE: In 1781, while Mozart was still employed by the Archbishop, he performed in the Sala Terrena – the oldest concert hall in Vienna

From his travels, Mozart already knew the principal singers, while the librettist Giambattista Varesco was court chaplain at Salzburg. In order to prepare *Idomeneo*, K366, Mozart was given a six-week leave of absence, although it would end up being four months before he returned to his post. During the period, he tailored his music to his singers, fusing their abilities and demands with his own ideas. The leading male roles are Prince Idamante (castrato soprano) and King Idomeneo (tenor). The latter role was performed by an experienced singer, the 66-year-old Anton Raaff, of whom Mozart wrote to his father: 'Raaff is the best and most faithful fellow in the world, but he is so set in his old routines that it would make your blood boil. As a result, it's very difficult to compose for him, though it's easy if you're willing to write conventional arias. Raaff is too fond of chopped noodles [display pieces] and pays no attention to expression.'

Idomeneo is a particularly important work because it is Mozart's first mature opera, achieving its unity through the imaginative deployment of traditional techniques. Set pieces such as arias and recitatives are treated with a new flexibility, while the role of the orchestra takes on a new importance. Mozart was writing for the famous Mannheim band, who had followed their employer Karl

> 'The composer must be allowed a free hand.' Wolfgang Amadeus Mozart, 1780

Theodor to Munich, and they, like the singers, expected to have opportunities to shine. Thus in its vocal and instrumental writing alike, *Idomeneo* represents a crucial stage in the development of opera, with characterisation and expression given a new priority. In Mozart's words, 'the composer must be allowed a free hand'. The ensemble opera had arrived.

Idomenco was first performed on 29 January 1781, two days after Mozart's 25th birthday. Leopold joined him for the occasion, and together they went on to visit their relatives in Augsburg, where Wolfgang received a formal summons from Archbishop Colloredo to come immediately to Vienna, where he and his court were then resident.

In March 1781, the Archbishop and his retinue had travelled to Vienna, where he was visiting his sick father, Prince Rudolf Joseph. Aside from the formalities of contract, it was important to Colloredo that Mozart should join him there, since he was the most attractive and famous musician in his employment.

Annoyed though he may have been by the summons, Mozart knew that Vienna was a city that held many opportunities for him, even though his previous visits to the city had been frustrating rather than satisfying; he had been paraded as a child prodigy in 1762 and the victim of theatre intrigues in 1769, while in 1773 his ten-week stay had fallen exactly when the aristocracy had retreated to their country estates. There were now many ▶

PLACE OF WORSHIP: Salzburg Cathedral was completely rebuilt in the Baroque style during the 17th century

acquaintances to meet once again, along with the possibility of meeting the Emperor and giving lucrative concert performances for the nobility.

Life with the Archbishop

When he arrived at Vienna, Mozart found that while his two musician colleagues, the violinist Brunetti and the castrato Francesco Ceccarelli, were free to live where they chose, he was instructed that he must live within the Archbishop's household. He was required to eat at table with the servants, which, although hardly remarkable, was something he bitterly resented after the freedom and respect he had enjoyed elsewhere. In a letter to Leopold he wrote: 'We lunch at about 12 o'clock, unfortunately somewhat early for me. Our party consists of the two valets, that is, the body and soul attendants of His Worship, the contrôleur, Herr Zetti, the confectioner, the two cooks, Ceccarelli, Brunetti, and my insignificant self. Note that the two valets sit at the top of the table, but at least I have the honour of being placed above the cooks. Well, I almost believe

myself back in Salzburg! A good deal of silly, coarse joking goes on at table, but no one cracks jokes with me, for I never say a word, or, if I have to speak, I always do so with the utmost gravity; and as soon as I have finished my munch, I get up and go off. We do not meet for supper, but we each receive three ducats, which goes a long way!'

It further angered Mozart when Colloredo refused him to perform at a charity concert and denied him the opportunity to engage in other private activities. He had to attend every formal visit the Archbishop undertook, waiting in an antechamber until required. That he resented this servitude is abundantly clear, and when he found himself at the residence of an old acquaintance, the Russian ambassador Prince Galitzin, he broke the bounds of this etiquette: 'When I went upstairs, Angelbauer (the Archbishop's valet) was on hand to tell the lackey to show me up. But I ignored their honours the valet and the lackey, and went straight through the rooms to the music room, as all the doors were open. And I went straight up to the

Prince and paid my respects. Then I stood talking with him. I had completely forgotten about Ceccarelli and Brunetti, for they were nowhere to be seen. They were tucked away behind the orchestra, against the wall, not daring to come forward.'

Out with a boot

These tensions continued for some two months, until Colloredo's patience snapped, and he rounded on Mozart, calling him a 'knave, rascal, dissolute fellow'. As for the composer, he felt little loyalty to his employer. Indeed, the two men represented in their determined attitudes the polarisation of the powerful social forces of the day. Mozart actively sought dismissal, and on 8 June 1781, unable to endure his rebellious behaviour any longer, the Archbishop instructed his Oberküchenmeister (Chamberlain), Count Arco, to physically remove the composer from the premises. Mozart's view of the affair was typically uncompromising: 'It is the heart that ennobles a man; and though I am no count, yet I have probably more honour in me than many a count. Whether a man be count or valet, the moment he insults me, he is a scoundrel.'

However, Count Arco was operating as more than simply the representative of Archbishop Colloredo, since for some weeks he had kept in close contact with Leopold Mozart, who resolutely insisted that his son should remain in his Salzburg post. To this end he wrote many letters to Wolfgang, and though these have not survived, the replies have, and it is clear that in making his decision to leave the Salzburg court to take up residence in Vienna, the son was seeking his independence from his father too: 'I implore you, dearest, most beloved father, to spare me such letters in the future. I entreat you to do so, for they only irritate my mind and disturb my heart and spirit; and I, who must now keep on composing, need a cheerful mind and a calm disposition.'

The Archbishop isn't entirely to blame for the break-up either. The main obligation of Salzburg composers was to write for the cathedral. While Mozart composed nine Masses between 1772 and 1777 as well as a dozen litanies and vespers, Michael Haydn, the other chief composer in Salzburg, wrote over 100 church works. Mozart's reluctance was obvious and the break-down in relations was inevitable.

Mozart was now a freelance musician in Vienna, free of all prior constraints for the last decade of his life. *Terry Barfoot* ∎

MOZART'S INFLUENCE

OPERATIC PERFORMANCE:
Dame Kiri Te Kanawa in the opening scene of Strauss's opera *Der Rosenkavalier*

Not only was Mozart popular with his contemporaries, especially Haydn, but his work has continued to inspire generations of composers including Mahler, Strauss and Schnittke

OF HIS CONTEMPORARIES, none admired Mozart more than Joseph Haydn, who left various statements recording his feelings. Beethoven, who settled in Vienna the year after Mozart's death, performed his music and was directly influenced by it in several works. For example, Beethoven composed cadenzas for Mozart's D minor Piano Concerto, K466, modelled his Quintet for Piano and Wind Instruments on Mozart's, and ingeniously made one of his *Diabelli* Variations turn into a treatment of a tune from *Don Giovanni*. The young Schubert modelled his quartets and symphonies on those of Mozart.

Those 19th century German composers who sought to proclaim the strength of the German tradition could hardly do so without acknowledging the importance of Mozart. Schumann, for instance, was never slow to do so in his writings and revered the classical tradition particularly in his chamber music, while Wagner acknowledged an admiration for *The Magic Flute* that links interestingly with his own style: 'Mozart is the founder of German declamation – what fine humanity resounds in the Priest's replies to Tamino!' Tchaikovsky always maintained that Mozart was his favourite composer, and he arranged some of the keyboard music into a suite, which he called *Mozartiana*.

It was during the 20th century that Mozart worship really rose to its greatest heights. Two great composer-conductors, Gustav Mahler and Richard Strauss, held him in special regard, and Strauss made his opera *Der Rosenkavalier* a tribute to 18th century Vienna, including many subtle pointers to *The Marriage of Figaro*. The French composers Jacques Ibert and Francis Poulenc paid creative homage to Mozart as well.

The trend continued into the 20th century. For example, Alfred Schnittke, one of the leading figures in contemporary music, received acclaim for his *Moz-Art*, composed in 1976. This piece shows how Mozart can directly generate a creative stimulus. Schnittke took an eight-bar fragment, K416d, and composed a virtuoso piece for two violins, a freely constructed fantasia that is more than a mere pastiche, also quoting the opening theme of the famous G minor Symphony towards the end. Schnittke described *Moz-Art* as 'loose leaves of an all-but-forgotten score by Mozart, which after nearly 200 years was heard in a miraculous way, by a most faithful pupil and devoted admirer'.

MOZART IN VIENNA

While he was in the capital, Mozart joined forces with the poet Lorenzo Da Ponte to write three immensely popular operas: *The Marriage of Figaro, Don Giovanni* and *Così fan tutte*

'I assure you that this is a splendid place, and for my talents the best one in the whole world.' So wrote Mozart to his father on 4 April 1781, soon after arriving in Vienna. Certainly the city offered opportunities to the ambitious musician; it had attracted Gluck a generation before, as it would attract the young Beethoven little more than a decade later. With a population of around 230,000, Vienna was by far the largest city in the German-speaking world, its thriving musical life centred on the domination of the court, which closely controlled the theatres staging the major performances.

> What Mozart wished to do above all was win the recognition of the Emperor Joseph II

Support of the aristocracy

Mozart was only 25 years old, but he was already an experienced composer with an international reputation, who had written widely in all the genres then current.

What's more, he believed in himself; he knew he had found his special identity as a musician. He was understandably anxious to display his creative talents, as well as his prowess as a performer, and as soon as he settled in Vienna, he was supported and encouraged by several aristocratic patrons. These included the Baroness Waldstätten, the Russian Ambassador, Count Galitzin, and Countess Wilhelmine Thun, the wife of Count Franz Joseph Thun, who had studied music with Haydn. Mozart reported to his father in March 1781 that she had already become a valuable ally to him: 'I've lunched twice already at Countess Thun's and go there almost every day – that's the most charming, the dearest lady I ever saw in my life; and she entertains a high opinion of me too. Her husband is still the same odd but well-intentioned and honourable gentleman.' ▶

GETTY

THE MASTER AT WORK:
During his time in Vienna,
Mozart composed some of
his best-known pieces

WEDDING BELLS: On 4 August 1782, Mozart married Constanze Weber. They had six children, but four died in infancy

SO MANY NOTES: A performance of *Die Entführung aus dem Serail* at the Royal Opera House in Berlin

However, what Mozart wished to do above all was win the recognition of the Emperor Joseph II. When he learned that there was an imperial band he immediately set about composing a wind sextet, but he had to hurriedly rework it for eight players instead of the original six, when he found he had miscalculated its size. This was the Serenade in E flat, K375, whose early performances Mozart described to his father: 'At 11 o'clock last night I was serenaded by two clarinets, two horns and two bassoons playing my own music; I had written it for St Theresa's Day for the sister-in-law of Herr von Hickel, the court painter, where it was performed for the first time. The six musicians are poor wretches who play together quite nicely all the same, especially the first clarinettist and the two horn players. But my chief reason for writing it was to let Herr von Strack (a Gentleman of the Emperor's Bed Chamber), who goes there every day, hear something of mine. And so I composed a

little bit reasonably. It was well received too and played in three different places on St Theresa's Night, because when they had finished it in one place they were taken somewhere else and paid to play it again. And so these musicians had the front gates opened for them, and when they had formed up in the yard, they gave me, just as I was about to undress for bed, the most delightful surprise in the world with the opening E flat chord.'

German opera

Mozart's most important opportunity to gain influence came with the German opera *Die Entführung aus dem Serail* (The abduction from the Seraglio), written for the short-lived *Nationalsingspiel* (German Opera) set up by the Emperor. It was perhaps a portent of the frustrations of musical life in Vienna that the premiere was delayed by ten months, but when it was eventually performed, the opera made a strong impression and remained Mozart's

most popular stage work throughout his lifetime. After the first performance, the Emperor famously commented, 'So many notes, my dear Mozart', to which the composer replied, 'Only as many as are needed, Your Majesty.'

The average *Singspiel*, with which Emperor Joseph II was making his comparison, was little more than a popular play, a sort of pantomime, interspersed with songs. But Mozart, with *Idomeneo* behind him, explored the plot of *Die Entführung* in a musical language that is far wider ranging both vocally and orchestrally than its predecessors in the tradition. The plot combines a popular Turkish setting – the Austrians loved to poke fun at the Ottoman Empire – with an attempted rescue motivated by love, and a resolution brought about by the generosity of the powerful Turkish pasha. In this way, the ideals of the Enlightenment add a deeper dimension, and the story blends the serious and the comic. Despite its success, in the main the

ANTONIO SALIERI

Born Legnago, Italy, 18 August 1750
Died Vienna, Austria, 7 May 1825

FOR ALL MOZART'S genius, during the 1780s, Viennese musical life was dominated by the Italian composer Antonio Salieri. Salieri gained notoriety through the dramatisation of his relationship with Mozart, firstly in a Pushkin play and its operatic adaptation by Rimsky-Korsakov, and then more recently in Peter Shaffer's play *Amadeus*, now a popular film. Though Salieri almost certainly did not poison Mozart, the two were definitely rivals, and the older man probably used his influence to obstruct the progress of Mozart's career.

Salieri was a very talented musician and composed his first opera at the age of 18. His gifts were recognised six years later when he was appointed a court composer and conductor of Italian opera in Vienna. By the time he was 38, he had risen to the position of Court Kapellmeister. He often worked with Lorenzo Da Ponte as his librettist, and his fame was international. Following the example of his lifelong friend Gluck, he became an important figure in Paris from around 1784, producing heroic operas to satisfy French taste and scoring his greatest triumph with the five-act *Tarare* (1787). The libretto was provided by Beaumarchais, and when Da Ponte made an Italian version, which was staged in Vienna the following year, it was styled an *opera tragicomica* and retitled *Axur, Re d'Ormus*.

In total Salieri wrote more than 40 operas, including the first setting of

Falstaff in 1799. His career was remarkably successful, but during the 1790s, his influence began to decline, and his operas gradually lost their prominence. His style seems formal in comparison with Mozart's ensemble operas. In the last phase of his career he retired from composition and turned instead to teaching, counting both Beethoven and Schubert among his pupils.

He never really changed his preference for the style he had known: 'Musical taste is gradually changing to a kind completely contrary to that of my own times; extravagance and confusion of styles have replaced rationality and majestic simplicity.'

From the historical point of view, his reputation suffers from the comparisons that are inevitably made. Yet to his contemporaries he was a master and arguably the leading musician of the day.

Viennese audience retained a preference for Italian opera. Therefore, at the first opportunity, Mozart turned to *opera buffa*.

At first, Mozart lodged with the Weber family, who had moved to Vienna from their previous home in Munich. This convenience was useful to him both financially and in terms of time. The cost and effort involved in keeping warm, cooking and other household chores was considerable, and would certainly have required – as it did later – the employment of servants. However, Leopold Mozart did not approve of the Webers, because he felt they were using his son for their own ends. There were four daughters, but by now the second, Aloysia, with whom Mozart had earlier fallen in love, had married and left home. What followed was probably inevitable – on 4 August 1782 he married Constanze, the third daughter, with his father's grudging consent.

Mozart and Constanze had six children, four of whom died in infancy. They often moved their accommodation, according to how his income related to their outgoings. It was fashionable but much more expensive to live in the centre of the city, and the most attractive lodgings were always on the third floor of buildings. This reflected the need to avoid the noise and smell of the street, in particular that of the many horses, but it was not too far to carry up firewood and the other necessities of life.

Mozart soon found that life in Vienna had its problems. His early concert promotions, including the first three Viennese piano concertos (nos. 11-13, K411-3), proved expensive, and in February 1783, he had to resort to asking for Baroness Waldstätten's help: 'If I do not repay the sum before tomorrow, he will bring an action against me. At the moment, I cannot pay, not even half the sum! If I could have foreseen that the subscriptions for my concerts would come in so slowly, I should have raised the money on a longer time limit. I entreat your ladyship for heaven's sake to help me keep my honour and my good name.'

Teaching and composing

During the Vienna years, Mozart created an astonishing stream of masterpieces. In 1784, his subscription series was particularly successful, and he responded by composing several piano concertos – in which he combined his prowess as a performer and composer – which were of a greater subtlety and quality than he had achieved hitherto and as such were ▶

LIFE IN THE CAPITAL: Both Mozart and Haydn lived near the New Market in Vienna, Austria

incredibly successful. On 3 March 1784, he wrote to his father: 'I shall give three subscription concerts in Trattner's Rooms, for which I already have 100 subscribers, and shall have another 30 by the time they start. I shall probably give two academy concerts in the theatre this year – so you can easily imagine that I am obliged to play new things – hence I must compose. The whole of the morning is devoted to pupils, and in the evening I must play in public almost every day.'

The most influential people in Vienna at that time were following Mozart, including the former Austrian Ambassador to Prussia, Baron Gottfried van Swieten. He was an enthusiast for the music of the great baroque masters, Bach and Handel, and at his regular musical gatherings, known as the *Gesellschaft der Assoziierten* (Society of Associates), he encouraged performances of this repertoire. Mozart observed: 'Every Sunday at noon I go to Baron von Suiten [sic] – and there nothing but Handel and Bach is played. I am making a collection of Bach fugues – not only

Sebastian's but Emanuel and Friedeman [sic] Bach's. Also Handel's.'

Mozart made performing editions of music by Bach and Handel, including *Messiah*, and in his own music his interest in Baroque style brought about important stylistic developments, particularly in relation to a greater reliance on counterpoint – the simultaneous presentation of ideas in a texture. This can be found, for instance, in the six string quartets he dedicated to his great contemporary Joseph Haydn. Around this time the two men became firm friends, and Mozart played the viola in string quartets with Haydn and two other talented composers, Jan Vanhal and Carl Ditters von Dittersdorf.

Joseph Haydn

Haydn had been in the employment of the Esterházy family since 1761, and during his time at the magnificent-but-remote palace of Esterháza in Hungary, his unique style developed. He remarked of his work at the palace: 'I was cut off,

and therefore forced to become original.' Haydn's musical development was one of the most extraordinary features in the evolution of the new classical style, and he proved to be a great influence on Mozart, whose music Haydn admired in turn. It was hearing Haydn's opus 33 string quartets that encouraged Mozart to return to the quartet medium, and he dedicated his set of quartets (K387, 421, 428, 458, 464 and 465) to the older composer: 'Most celebrated man and very dear friend, take these six children of mine. They are, indeed, the fruit of long and laborious toil. During your last stay in this capital, you, yourself, my very dear friend, expressed your pleasure in these compositions. Your approval encourages me to offer them to you and leads me to hope that you will not find them wholly unworthy of your favour. Please receive them kindly and be a father, guide and friend to them!'

Haydn understood well enough the quality of these pieces. He told Leopold Mozart, who was staying in Vienna in 1785: 'I tell you before God, and as an

GETTY, ALAMY

Mozart und Haydn

FRIENDLY ADVICE: Haydn's original musical style had a big influence on Mozart

honest man, that your son is the greatest composer I know, either personally or by reputation; he has taste and moreover the greatest knowledge of the science of composing.'

While in Vienna, Leopold Mozart wrote back to his daughter in Salzburg, describing the frenzied nature of life when his son was enjoying periods of success: 'We never go to bed before one o'clock and I never get up before nine. We lunch at two or half past. The weather is horrible. Every day there are concerts; and the whole time is given up to teaching, music, composing and so forth. I feel rather out of it all. If only the concerts were over! It is impossible for me to describe the rush and bustle. Since my arrival your brother's fortepiano has been taken at least a dozen times to the theatre or to some other house.'

Like Mozart, both van Swieten and Haydn were Freemasons. In December 1784, Mozart was initiated as an 'Entered Apprentice' of the lodge *Zur Wolthäkigkeit* (Beneficence), and he soon found that he enjoyed the comradeship of his fellow

> 'I tell you before God, and as an honest man, that your son is the greatest composer I know.'
> Haydn to Leopold Mozart

masons. Their ideals of humanity, tolerance and brotherhood matched his own. He composed a considerable amount of music for the various Viennese lodges, but in due course Emperor Joseph II became suspicious of Freemasons and, under pressure from the Church, placed severe restrictions on their activities.

The heart of opera

Throughout his life, opera remained Mozart's creative priority. After *Die Entführung*, two *buffa* operas – *L'oca del Cairo* (The Goose of Cairo) and *Lo sposo deluso* (The Deluded Bridegroom) were begun and abandoned. But *opera buffa*, which offered the chance to characterise real people rather than stock types,

remained the opportunity he sought. Vienna was a major operatic centre, and although the Imperial theatres were dominated by Kapellmeister Antonio Salieri, activity was such that a wide range of operas were performed. One that Mozart particularly admired was a new *opera buffa* by Giovanni Paisiello, *The Barber of Seville*, which was based on a contemporary play by the Baron de Beaumarchais. He was therefore attracted to the idea of writing an opera on that play's sequel, *The Marriage of Figaro*.

Mozart probably knew the play through the recent German translation by his friend Emanuel Schikaneder, but the Emperor had banned its performance on the grounds that the plot was seditious, since it undermined the social standing ▶

MOZART'S FAMILY:
CONSTANZE AND THE CHILDREN

After an unsuccessful first love, Mozart found happiness in his marriage

CONSTANZE MOZART (1762-1842) was the third of the four daughters of Fridolin Weber (1733-79), a singer, violinist and copyist at the Mannheim court, and his wife Maria Caecilia (1727-93). Mozart first encountered the Weber family at Mannheim when he stopped there while en route to Paris during the winter of 1777-78. He fell in love with the second eldest daughter, Aloysia, but when he visited Mannheim on his return several months later, he found to his dismay that she had lost interest in him.

After Fridolin died in 1779, the remaining members of the family moved first to Munich and then to Vienna, where Aloysia, a talented singer, had gained an operatic engagement. Mozart encountered them again in 1781, and was fortunate that after he decided to settle in the city, they were able to offer him accommodation. This was particularly helpful during the period he was establishing his position there as he was able to save time and money by living with the family.

Despite the opposition of his father, who felt that Frau Weber was pushing his son into an inappropriate liaison, Mozart married Constanze in 1782. They had six children, of whom only two survived infancy: Carl Thomas (1784-1858) and Franz Xaver Wolfgang (1791-1844). The remaining children were Raimund Leopold (1783-83), Johann Thomas Leopold (1786-86), Theresia (1787-88) and Anna Maria (1789-89).

Mozart's letters reveal that he relied both materially and emotionally on Constanze, and was lonely when away from her. Some writers have been less than generous to her, claiming that she was capricious and unreliable. However, such an interpretation seems at odds with the efficiency with which she acted after Mozart's death, when she dealt with his estate and encouraged performances of his works, in which she sometimes sang herself. In 1809, Constanze married Georg Nissen, helping him to write a biography of Mozart. They settled in Salzburg, where she remained after his death in 1826.

SISTER ACT: Constanze wa not Mozart's first love; he ha previously wooed her siste

BROTHERS IN ARMS: Carl Thomas and Franz Xaver Wolfgang Mozart

---

of the aristocracy. The Viennese court poet, Lorenzo da Ponte, with whom Mozart now collaborated, overcame this official opposition by adapting his libretto with the utmost guile and cunning. In *The Marriage of Figaro*, the Mozart-Da Ponte collaboration created a range of characters of a depth and subtlety hitherto unknown in opera. There is wit and tenderness, as well as serious comment about human nature; in the words of the writer Stendhal: 'All the characters are turned towards the tender or the passionate. Mozart's opera is a sublime blend of wit and melancholy which is without any parallel.'

Yet Mozart experienced difficulties with the work. Leopold Mozart heard about them from some friends, the Duschek family, who had recently been in Vienna, and he wrote about it to his daughter: 'Today your brother's opera, *The Marriage of Figaro*, will be staged for the first time. It will be remarkable if it succeeds, for I know that extraordinary cabals have been mounted against him. Salieri with his followers have set heaven and earth in motion yet again to

defeat him, because he has gained such a great reputation through his special talent and cleverness.'

A fresh triumph
Figaro enjoyed more success in Prague than it had in Vienna, and Mozart was invited there at the beginning of 1787 to conduct it. He wrote back to a Viennese friend, Gottfried von Jacquin: 'I looked on with the greatest pleasure while all these people flew about in sheer delight to the music of my *Figaro*, arranged for quadrilles and waltzes. For here they talk about nothing but *Figaro*. No opera is pulling the crowds like *Figaro*. Nothing, nothing but *Figaro*. Certainly a great honour for me.'

Pasquale Bondini, the manager of the Estates Theatre in Prague, commissioned Mozart to write a new opera for a fee of 100 gulden. Since composers only received fees from commissions or special benefit performances, this was a great opportunity, and the result was the second Da Ponte collaboration, *Don Giovanni*. A third would follow in Vienna in 1790: *Così fan tutte*.

An important part of Mozart's income was derived from his piano pupils. From his childhood his reputation had been international, and in 1787 the authorities in the Rhineland principality of Bonn sent a talented 17 year old to play to him: Ludwig van Beethoven. Although there is no clear evidence that formal lessons took place, Mozart did hear Beethoven perform at the keyboard, and observed of the young talent: 'Watch out for him, he will have something to say.' However, the young man's mother became ill, and he had to return to Bonn.

Another of Mozart's pupils during 1787 was Johann Nepomuk Hummel, who later became a celebrated pianist and composer. He recalled: 'Mozart was of a small build, and his face was pale. His countenance contained much that was pleasant and friendly, combined with something of a melancholy seriousness; his large blue eyes gleamed brightly. In a circle of good friends he could also be quite merry, lively and witty; sometimes he could be sarcastic!'

MODERN PERFORMANCE: In 1787, Mozart's opera *Don Giovanni* premiered at the Estates Theatre in Prague. Over 200 years later, it is as popular as ever

COMIC TIMING: A scene from *The Marriage of Figaro*. The opera was the first of three collaborations between Mozart and Da Ponte

This view was confirmed by Michael Kelly, who worked with the composer as an opera singer in Vienna: 'He was a remarkably small man, very thin and pale, with a profusion of fine hair, of which he was rather vain. He gave me a cordial invitation to his house, of which I availed myself, and passed a great deal of my time there. He always received me with kindness and hospitality. He was remarkably fond of punch, of which beverage I have seen him take copious draughts. He was also fond of billiards, and had an excellent billiard table in his house. Many and many a game have I played with him, but always came off second best. He gave Sunday concerts, at which I was never missing.'

Of his many pupils Mozart held the young Englishman Thomas Attwood in particular regard: 'Attwood is a young man for whom I have a sincere affection and esteem; he conducts himself with great propriety, and I feel much pleasure in telling you, that he

partakes more of my style than any scholar I ever had. I predict that he will prove a sound musician.'

Despite his numerous successes during his Vienna years, Mozart's circumstances were often precarious. His lifestyle was expensive – after all, he had to move in aristocratic circles – but his income was not constant. His subscription concerts, for instance, went in and out of fashion, and suffered also from the fluctuations of economic and political developments. Furthermore, the death his father in 1787

> The economy collapsed, and the members of the nobility – Mozart's core support – were either involved in running the war campaign, or chose to conserve their resources

affected him deeply, and indeed, from this point on there is an intensification of emotion in many of Mozart's works, in particular those adopting minor keys, such as the String Quintet, K516, or the Symphony No. 40, K550.

During the last few years of his life, his financial position was often critical, and he resorted to borrowing money from friends, in particular his fellow Freemason, the merchant Michael Puchberg. Throughout these years Mozart sought a prestigious court appointment, but his only such role

PREMIER LOCATION: The Austrian National Theatre in Vienna opened on 14 March 1741. Three of Mozart's operas premiered here

was nominal, that of Kammermusicus (Chamber Musician), involving the composition of dance music only. Viennese musical life was competitive, and intrigues sometimes impeded his progress. War with the Ottoman Empire and Emperor Joseph II's death in 1790 also limited the scale of musical activity during this period.

War with the Ottoman Empire

The war, which was enthusiastically welcomed by the Viennese when it began, soon went badly, and it proved disastrous for Mozart. The economy collapsed, and the members of the nobility, who represented the composer's core support, were either involved directly in running the campaign, or chose to conserve their resources. By 1788, Mozart and Constanze were living beyond their means and were accumulating severe debts.

The last three symphonies, composed in the summer of 1788 when the Mozarts moved to the suburb of Wahring, were probably intended for a projected series of subscription concerts to take place at the Casino. They probably had to be cancelled for lack of support. Thus it was that through the last years of his life Mozart wrote a series of letters to Puchberg, asking for help, which was generously given. In one of them he admits that his opportunities are insufficient: 'I beg you to lend me until tomorrow at least a couple of hundred gulden, as my landlord at the Landstrasse has been so importunate that in order to avoid an unpleasant incident I have had to pay him on the spot, and this has made things awkward for me! We are sleeping tonight, for the first time, in our new quarters, where we shall remain both summer and winter. On the whole the change is all the same to me – in fact I prefer it. As it is, I have very little to do in town, and as I am not exposed to so many visitors, I shall have more time for work.

Moreover, our rooms are now cheaper...' The difficulties in Vienna led Mozart to consider other possibilities. In 1789, between April and June, he travelled north with Prince Lichnowsky, visiting Dresden, Leipzig and Berlin, where he entertained vague hopes of a court appointment. The following year, he received an offer to go to London to give opera performances, but he did not act on it.

Mozart, anxious as ever to please a new ruler, travelled to Frankfurt in September 1790 for the coronation of Leopold II. Leopold had succeeded his brother Joseph to the Austrian throne after the latter died of pneumonia at the age of 48. Leopold's entourage, travelling with him on this auspicious occasion, was impressive: 1,493 cavalrymen, 1,336 foot soldiers, and 15 musicians under the direction of Kapellmeister Salieri. Mozart went to Frankfurt privately and by his own choice; nothing conclusive resulted. *Terry Barfoot* ■

THE FINAL YEAR

Following a serious illness, Mozart died at the age of 35.
However, up until his last moments he continued to compose,
instructing others when he was no longer well enough to write himself

After a period of much frustration and hardship, 1791 brought new challenges and opportunities. Mozart's major works alone included two operas, the final piano concerto, No. 27 in B flat, K595, the E flat String Quintet, K614, the Clarinet Concerto, K622, and the Requiem. The pressures of having to keep to schedule must have contributed to his poor health and, of course, there were also the pressing needs of his young family.

In June, he visited Constanze at the nearby spa of Baden, where, eight months pregnant, she was taking the cure. For the choirmaster there, Anton Stoll, he composed the beautiful motet *Ave verum*, K618. Then, shortly after he had returned

LAST NOTES: This portrait of Mozart composing the Requiem was painted by William James Grant in 1854

to Vienna, he received a commission from an anonymous messenger, requesting him to compose a Requiem.

A last commission

Count Franz Walsegg-Stuppach's young wife, Anna, had died in February 1791, and he decided to honour her memory by commissioning a setting of the Requiem Mass. It was the Count's habit to stage music soirées at his home, and sometimes to suggest that he might be the composer of the new music his guests heard. So it was that Walsegg sent his steward to Mozart with the commission for the Requiem. It was probably because he received payment in advance that Mozart accepted the Requiem commission,

---

'There was not a single number that did not call forth from him a bravo! Or a bello!' Mozart on Salieri, 14 October 1791

---

at a time when he was already heavily committed; especially to his two operas *La clemenza did Tito* and *Die Zauberflöte*. Therefore, he did not begin work in earnest on the Requiem until October.

The *opera seria La clemenza di Tito* was a commission to celebrate the coronation of Leopold II as King of Bohemia; Salieri had been approached first but had declined on grounds of existing commitments. In August, Mozart travelled to Prague to supervise the rehearsals, and he took with him his pupil Franz Süssmayr and his clarinettist friend Anton Stadler, for whom he wrote several *obbligato* numbers. A few weeks later, he rewarded Stadler further with the Clarinet Concerto, K622.

In September, on returning to Vienna, Mozart completed the *Singspiel Die Zauberflöte* (The Magic Flute), which the actor, singer and impresario Schikaneder had commissioned in the spring, for performance at Theater auf der Wieden. This opera contains the widest stylistic range to be found in any of Mozart's works, with aspects of popular song for the bird-catcher Papageno, *opera seria* display for the Queen of the Night, deeply felt, noble music for the hero Tamino, and solemn, profound pronouncements for the mystical ▶

MOZART'S WOMEN

Behind every great man is a great woman – or women in Mozart's case. **Chris de Souza** *reveals the composer's leading ladies*

MARIE ANTOINETTE:
Archduchess of Austria
and Queen of France

Mozart met Marie Antoinette, not normally reckoned a pivotal figure in his life, during his first visit to the Austrian court: he was six, she a year older. Her mother, Maria Theresa, had relaxed court protocol, so it was permissible for her to lift the boy onto her lap. It's rumoured that Mozart was quite taken with the future Queen and even promised to marry her. Later as Queen of France, music lover though she was, she did nothing to help Mozart when he visited Paris, Gluck then being in her close circle.

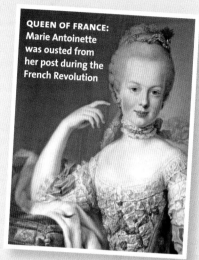

QUEEN OF FRANCE: Marie Antoinette was ousted from her post during the French Revolution

CONSTANZE WEBER

Mozart met his future wife when he lodged with her family in Vienna in 1781. Leopold disapproved, but young love triumphed. They eventually moved in together, and married to avoid scandal. They shared an enjoyable sex life, and had six children, only two of whom survived. Constanze's influence on Mozart was profound. A fine singer, her skill is reflected in the soprano part of the C minor Mass, and she encouraged Mozart to study Bach's fugues and compose his own. After Mozart's death, she worked hard to preserve his heritage, had many works published and wrote his first biography.

YOUNG LOVE: Mozart composed many pieces for Aloysia Weber

ALOYSIA WEBER

Mozart met and fell in love with his future sister-in-law on tour in Mannheim in 1777. To scupper the affair, Mozart's father ordered him to Paris. When they next met, she no longer wanted him. According to Constanze, he sat at the piano and sang 'Leek mir das Mensch im Arsch, das mich nicht will' ('The one who doesn't want me can lick my arse'). They met again in 1781 when Mozart lodged with her mother. He composed much for her, including *Popoli di Tessaglia*, with the highest vocal note in the classical repertoire. She sang Donna Anna in the Vienna premiere of *Don Giovanni* in 1788.

NANCY STORACE

Storace became a member of the Vienna Court where as a 20-year-old she created the role of Susanna in *Figaro*. If the music he wrote for her is anything to go by, her relationship with Mozart was very close. When she returned to England he composed 'Ch'io mi scordi di te?', a duet for soprano, piano and orchestra, with Mozart himself playing the piano part at her farewell concert, and no doubt relishing the intertwining of piano and vocal lines. The words at the end speak for themselves: 'Fear nothing, my beloved, my heart will always be yours.'

DEATH BED: Herman von Kaulbach created this painting of Mozart's last moments in 1878

leader Sarastro and his followers. The orchestra contains trombones and gives special emphasis to the rich tone of basset horns, while the imagery – surrounding the search to attain a higher order of humanity – is clearly Masonic.

His final work

Die Zauberflöte was received with much enthusiasm, not least by Salieri, as Mozart informed his wife, who was again at Baden: 'At six o'clock I called in the carriage for Salieri and Madame Cavalieri, and drove them to my box. You can hardly imagine how charming they were and how much they liked not only my music, but also the libretto and everything. They both said that it was an operone, worthy to be performed for the grandest festival and before the greatest monarch, and that they would often go to see it, as they had never seen a more beautiful or delightful show. Salieri listened and watched most attentively, and from the overture to the last chorus there was not a single number that did not call forth from him a bravo! Or a bello!

> Despite his financial troubles, Mozart was held in high esteem at the time of his death

It seemed as if they could not thank me enough for my kindness.'

In November, Mozart, who was prone to bouts of depression, was cheered by the performance of his *Kleine Freimaurer-Kantate* (Little Masonic Cantata, K623). He was now hard at work on the Requiem, but was ill and behind schedule. His condition worsened and he was bedridden from the end of November, though he still composed. He gave Süssmayr instructions about his plans, as he was unable to complete the task himself, and he died on 5 December 1791. The cause of his death remains a matter of conjecture, though the most likely suggestion is that he suffered from uraemia, brought on by kidney failure. Whatever his precise condition, the traditional treatment he received – bleeding by leeches – surely hastened his demise.

Despite his financial troubles, the obituary notices prove that Mozart was held in high esteem at the time of his death. Had he enjoyed a normal lifespan, he would still have been active well into the next century; and since he died at 35 it is misleading to apply the term 'late' to any of his works.

Legacy

Mozart gave music a new enlightenment and humanistic spirit, and his friend and fellow composer Joseph Haydn recognised that in him all musical trends seemed to meet: 'If only I could impress on the soul of every friend of music how inimitable are Mozart's works, how musically intelligent, how extraordinarily sensitive.' Mozart was, and remains, the most universal of composers. *Terry Barfoot* ■

GETTY X2

A PAUPER'S GRAVE

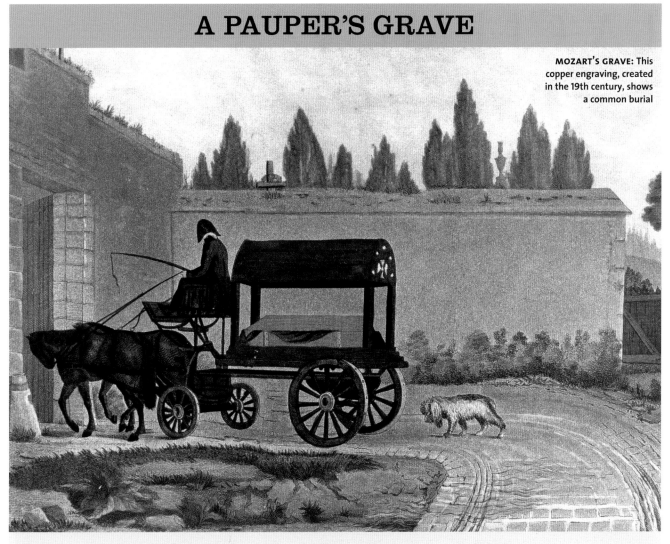

MOZART'S GRAVE: This copper engraving, created in the 19th century, shows a common burial

Fact or fiction? Did the famous composer really end up in a common grave?

ONE OF THE MOST popular myths about Mozart is that he was buried in a pauper's grave. But was he? There is no direct evidence concerning the funeral and burial, therefore the best way to consider what actually happened is by reference to the normal procedures of the time.

The service took place in a small chapel within St Stephen's Cathedral, but the number of mourners and the nature of the service are unknown. Under the reforms of Emperor Joseph II during the 1780s, extravagance at funerals was discouraged, but even if the funeral itself was low-key, Mozart's death hardly went unnoticed. His masonic lodge held a 'Lodge of Sorrows' in his memory, while a memorial service in Prague attracted no fewer than 4,000 mourners. The prevailing regulations insisted that only after six o'clock in the evening (nine in summer) could the coffin

be transported to the cemetery, in order to minimise risks to the public during epidemics. There were no ceremonies held at the graveside, and priests were seldom present, only the gravedigger and his assistants. Friends and family sometimes attended, but the journey was difficult after dark and on 8 December 1791, the evening in question, there was a storm raging. The cemetery of St Marx was in the Landstrasse district, some three miles from the cathedral, and the hearse would hardly have moved at a stately pace, particularly in view of the weather. Therefore any mourners would have had to hire a carriage of their own, since the walking distance was in excess of an hour. The coffin would have been kept overnight in a small mortuary, ready for burial the next morning. Emperor Joseph II had recommended reusable coffins and burials in sacks, but this regulation

was relaxed after many complaints from families. However, the practice remained widespread, though in Mozart's case the funeral expenses were paid by Gottfried van Swieten and take account of the cost of a coffin. Communal graves, generally containing around four bodies, were the norm, and gravestones were only permitted around the cemetery walls. The surroundings were bleak, with only a few trees or bushes between the gravesites.

The first biography of Mozart, completed in 1828 by Constanze and her second husband Georg Nikolaus von Nissen, encouraged the myth: 'Mozart's mortal remains were buried in the cemetery of St Marx just outside Vienna. Because Swieten took into consideration the greatest possible economy for the family, the coffin was deposited in a common grave and every other expense avoided.'

LA CLEMENZA DI TITO

Metropolitan Opera, New York, 1984. Dir. Jean-Pierre Ponnelle

Singers rehearse for a performance of *La clemenza di Tito*. Set in Rome in AD 79, the new Emperor Tito finds himself a target for assassination.

GETTY

FORMAL ATTIRE: Mozart in court dress aged seven, shortly before he embarked on his grand tour of Europe

A life in 10 *masterpieces*

Hilary Finch explores the short but colourful
life of Mozart, through his greatest musical accomplishments

The ups and downs of Mozart's life are shown throughout his extensive repertoire. From the triumphant Symphony No. 25 in G minor, reflecting a new passion flowing through his life and work, to the sombre and emotive Requiem that Mozart worked on until his untimely death. During his time with the Archbishop, Mozart created some fabulous church music, especially the *Coronation* Mass. Of course, he is famous for his operas, which are as popular now as when they were written. On top of all this, Mozart wrote a wealth of orchestral pieces, composed for friends and clients, along with some remarkably mature pieces from his childhood. Choosing just 10 top pieces from his plethora of work is no mean feat...

1 *Keyboard Sonata in C for four hands, K19d*

WHEN THE MOZART family reaches London in 1764, Wolfgang meets Johann Christian Bach, the youngest son of Johann Sebastian, and they improvise together. This meeting has far-reaching influences on Mozart's writing, both on his early symphonies and his piano concertos.

JC Bach is a champion of the new fortepiano, and it is at his concerts that the pre-Classical piano concerto becomes the most fashionable of genres. It is said that nobody could tell at a first hearing whether a new piano work was by the young Mozart, or by JC himself. It is the blending of Italian melody with Northern European harmonic and textural thoroughness of composition that Mozart finds irresistibly stimulating as a model. Mozart loves London and England: later in life he will learn the language, and describe himself as an 'arch-Englishman'. The gem of his London compositions is the C major Sonata for piano duet, which is probably performed for the first time with his sister on 13 May 1765. Not only does it have all the virtuoso tricks Leopold would have demanded – such as echo effects and plenty of hand-crossing – but it also breathes keenly and eagerly with a spirit of real independence. Something new is going on here – so much so that some commentators have wondered if it is in fact a later work, suggesting the crafty Leopold may have fiddled with the date.

Sudden rhythmic gear changes disrupt the opening *Allegro*, and the scholar Wolfgang Hildesheimer has reflected on a certain disarming and entirely Mozartean sense of tender innocence: 'a peculiar, gentle, soothing magic', which hangs over the entire work.

RECOMMENDED RECORDING

Jenö Jandó (piano), Zsuzsa Kollar (piano)
Naxos 8.553518

A FRESH TAKE: Annick Massis takes the role of Giurnia and Roberzo Sacca plays Lucio Silla in this performance of the opera

2 *Lucio Silla, K135*

COMPOSED DURING MOZART'S third and last Italian journey, *Lucio Silla* represents a great leap forward, and is by far his most significant early opera.

Lucio Silla receives 26 performances following its premiere in December 1772 – and the lead castrato of the opera, Venanzio Rauzzini, inspires the great solo motet *Exsulate, jubilate*, written in January 1773. For *Lucio Silla*, Mozart composes the choruses, overture and recitative well in advance, waiting to write the arias until he met the soloists: one of them turns up just eight days before the first night!

Lucio Silla was a bloodthirsty tyrant who conquered Greece and made a treaty with Mitridate himself. In the opera, he tries to woo Senator Cecilio's bride Giunia, who hopes to free her country from Silla's yoke. She rejects a suggestion to marry Silla in order to murder him: Cecilio steps in, and is imprisoned. Giunia is ready to die with Cecilio, but Silla forgives everyone, and abdicates. The 17-year-old Mozart now movingly identifies with his characters. And, although many of the arias may seem long and busy, the virtuoso writing does express deeply moving emotions. Giunia's 'Fra i pensier pili funesti' is an early example of Mozart's C minor mood, with his beloved divided violas.

There's even a formidable trio ('Quell'orgoglioso sdegno'), which, in its simultaneous expression of differing emotions, foreshadows the great quartet *Idomeneo*. The chorus's dark scenes reveal Mozart's admiration for the work of Gluck, who had met and encouraged him in Vienna.

RECOMMENDED RECORDING

Henriette Bonde-Hansen (soprano), Susanne Elmark (soprano), Kristina Hammarström (mezzo soprano), Jakob Næslund Madsen (tenor), Simone Nold (soprano), Lothar Odinius (tenor) & Richard Lewis (harpsichord); Danish Radio Sinfonietta & Ars Nova Copenhagen/Adam Fischer
Dacapo 8226069-71

3 *Symphony No. 25 in G minor, K183*

WITH HIS MIND and spirit seething with the impressions and influences of all the musicians he had met throughout Europe, in the summer of 1773, Mozart meets Haydn in Vienna. An intensification in every area of his writing is sensed from now on: string quartets and symphonies pour out of the barely 18-year-old Mozart. It is both over-easy and under accurate to say that this 'little' G minor Symphony is a pre-echo of Mozart's 'great' one, No. 40.

Doubtless spurred on by Haydn's Symphony No. 39 in the same key, and fired by his encounters with his music, Mozart finds a new urgency within syncopation, a new daring in the dramatic falling diminished sevenths, a strengthening of harmonic direction, and echo effects that really ratchet up the tension. Does this music stem from a first, passionate love affair? References in letters to Mozart's sister do lead to this suggestion.

Or is Mozart already perfectly well aware of the emotional charge of keys such as G minor and E flat? And is he simply channelling his musically impassioned energies into the cutting-edge style of *Sturm und Drang*, currently raging through German literature and Austrian music? Whatever the stimuli and inspiration for this work, it remains an early masterpiece that can thrill in even a mediocre performance.

RECOMMENDED RECORDING

The Danish National Chamber Orchestra/Adam Fischer
Dacapo 6220542

GETTY X2

4 'Coronation' Mass in C, K317

THE FIRST SUBSTANTIAL work on Mozart's return to Salzburg in 1779 – and his finest Salzburg mass – is composed for the ceremonial Papal crowning of an image of the Blessed Virgin Mary in a church near Salzburg. The *Coronation* Mass still counts as a Missa brevis (he had already penned several, church dignitaries never wanted the music to hang about) but this mass is both gloriously expansive and tauter in structure than any of its predecessors. Of all Mozart's masses, it's probably the one most frequently performed both by church choirs and in professional secular concerts.

The symphonic drive of the Credo is unexpectedly broken off for a breathtakingly slow 'Et incarnates est' – isolating and glorifying the humanity of Christ, touching on distant keys, and haloed with delicate violin arabesques. The soprano solo in the 'Agnus dei' seems irresistibly a pre-echo of the Countess's 'Dove sono' in *Figaro*: she, too, knew a little of what it was like to be a potential sacrificial lamb.

RECOMMENDED RECORDING

Susan Gritton (soprano), Frances Bourne (mezzo-soprano), Sam Furness (tenor) & George Humphreys (bass); Choir of St John's College, Cambridge & St John's Sinfonia/Andrew Nethsingha
Chandos CHAN0786

RELIGIOUS WORK: The *Coronation* Mass was first performed at The Church of Maria Plain, near Salzburg

5 Idomeneo, K366

WHILE STILL IN the pay of the Archbishop of Salzburg, during the summer of 1780, Mozart receives a commission to write an opera for Munich, where the Elector of Mannheim had moved his court.

The Elector and his Mannheim singers want a serious, Italian opera – just the sort of specification for which Mozart is after. The subject of King Idomeneus of Crete was previously told through Andre Campra's opera of 1712. The tale was to be reworked for Mozart by a Salzburg chaplain, Gianbattista Varesco. Mozart cannily suggests that the opera be constructed after the French manner (with plenty of ensembles and choral and ballet set-pieces) – and begins writing at home in Salzburg in October 1780. He leaves Salzburg for Munich on 5 November – not to return until the following March, so long and successful is *Idomeneo*'s run. But the opera is not quickly taken up by other opera houses.

Although it can well be considered the greatest *opera seria* ever written, this form of serious, classically inspired drama per musica was by now becoming unfashionable, and many changes are made for a subsequent 1786 performance in Vienna.

Richard Strauss famously championed the work, making his own version in 1931, with great missionary zeal and not a little self-interest. His affectionate score was successfully presented at the 2010 Buxton Festival. But it was Fritz Busch's conducting of the 1951 Glyndebourne production that really re-established *Idomeneo*.

Now we can't get enough of it. And no wonder: it remains one of Mozart's supreme achievements. His Mannheim players inspire orchestral music of ravishing imagination – Ilia's aria, 'Se il padre perdei' was re-written at the last minute with four *obbligato* woodwinds, to celebrate his colleagues' prowess.

And here, too, the composer's beloved clarinets appear, delectably, for the first time in an opera. Mozart's intense engagement with the plight of father, son, the exiled, the abandoned and the jealous is concentrated not only in matchless arias, but in recitatives that are taut with drama. And in ensembles, too – crowned by the quartet 'Andro ramingo e solo', in which the feelings of four characters are presented simultaneously: the bravery of Idamames; the revenging desires of Elettra; the sadness of Ilia; and the pious terror of Idomeneo himself. Beethoven's quartet from *Fidelio* could surely not have been born without this musical midwife. Indeed, the Mozart commentator and critic William Mann considers *Idomeneo* as 'an upbeat to *Fidelio* and *The Ring*'.

RECOMMENDED RECORDING

Ian Bostridge (tenor), Lorraine Hunt Lieberson (tenor), Lisa Milne (soprano), Barbara Frittoli (soprano), Anthony Rolfe Johnson (tenor); Scottish Chamber Orchestra/Sir Charles Mackerras
EMI 948 2382

7 The Marriage of Figaro, K492

WHILE WRITING THE D minor Piano Concerto, Mozart has other things on his mind. Beaumarchais' play, *Le Mariage de Figaro*, is Paris' hot ticket in 1784, and a German version is printed in Vienna, despite the play's politically and socially contentious subject matter. In Austria, it is banned as a play, but what if it is sung instead?

Not surprisingly, this audacious and inflammatory, topsy-turvy, upstairs-downstairs play is just the sort of thing for which Mozart has been searching since Christmas 1782, when Count Orsini Rosenberg invited him to compose a new *opera buffa* for Vienna. What's more, Mozart has recently met Lorenzo Da Ponte, one of the staff court poets, who offered to collaborate with him. And Mozart, who knows that Da Ponte has succeeded with librettos based on French plays about real characters – not *commedia dell'arte* masks – welcomed the offer. Da Ponte's brilliant distillation of the long and elaborate play is the first – some would say the greatest – of his collaborations with Mozart. Work begins in earnest in October 1785, and *The Marriage of Figaro* premieres on May Day 1786 at Vienna's Burgtheater. Many numbers are applauded and encored at the first three performances, and the opera is revived for 26 performances between 1789-90.

RECOMMENDED RECORDING

Terfel, Gilfry, Hagley, Martinpelto; Monteverdi Choir, English Baroque Soloists/Sir John Eliot Gardiner
Archiv 439 8712

6 Piano Concerto No. 20 in D minor, K466

THE SERIES OF piano concertos Mozart writes in Vienna are surely his greatest achievements in instrumental music, taking the form way beyond the concertos of his predecessors and contemporaries in thematic richness, and in the subtlety and daring of the constantly developing relationship between soloist and orchestra. No concerto of Mozart's is better known than No. 20, composed in 1785. And it glories, too, in Beethoven's cadenzas, which are almost sacrosanct. Here, for the first time, there is no well-defined theme, ripe for the soloist to take up on his entry. This concerto, with its altogether more sophisticated relationship between the orchestra and the soloist, gives the soloist an entirely new theme – which appears all of 77 bars after the smouldering syncopations of the orchestra in pleading, pathos-timed phrases, which could almost be vocal. Mozart develops every new turn of phrase with such cunning that commentators' attempts at analysis tend to resemble pages of algebra. The Romanza (a word increasingly attractive to Mozart in his later years) is a true aria of a slow movement, leaping from one register to another, embroidered by dark orchestral textures, and followed by a hastily written, adrenalin-fuelled *Rondo finale* of kaleidoscopic orchestral composition.

RECOMMENDED RECORDING

Maria-João Pires (piano); Orchestra Mozart/Claudio Abbado
Deutsche Grammophon 479 0075

The unknown Mozart

*So you think you know your Wolfgang? Misha Donat uncovers
10 works you might not have heard before*

'Ch'io mi scordi di te?', K505

Mozart's concert-arias are a treasure trove of neglected masterpieces. 'Ch'io mi scordi di te?' is actually an aria and miniature piano concerto rolled into one, showing us just how closely related are the worlds of Mozart's operas and concertos.

Davide penitente, K469

Mozart salvaged the music of his great unfinished Mass in C minor, K427, by turning it into an oratorio with new words, and adding two spectacular arias. The music itself places grand Handelian choruses cheek by jowl with passages in operatic style.

Adagio & Rondo in C minor, K617

The most ethereally beautiful of the shorter pieces Mozart composed at the end of his life combines the unique sound of the glass armonica with a quartet consisting of flute, oboe, viola and cello.

Sonata in F major for piano duet, K497

This grandest of all Mozart's piano duets is in effect a symphony in disguise, complete with an imposing slow introduction. The last two movements, in particular, find Mozart revelling in his contrapuntal mastery.

Adagio for two clarinets & three basset horns, K411

The mellow sound of clarinets and their lower-pitched cousins called basset-horns gives Mozart's wind writing a special character. This piece scored for them has a velvety sonority that lends the music a nostalgic quality.

Fantasia in F minor, K608

One in a small group of pieces for a mechanical organ, that Mozart wrote in his last year. Its intense and dramatic outer sections enclose a middle section in the form of a serene series of variations.

Suite for piano, K399

In 1782, Mozart became fascinated by Bach and Handel. He completed no more than the Overture, Allemande and Courante of this Baroque-style suite, but they stand comparison with the corresponding movements in Bach's Partitas and English Suites.

Zaide, K344

This *Singspiel*, a forerunner of *Die Entführung aus dem Serail*, was left incomplete, but it's full of great music. Mozart's use of melodrama – music interspersed with spoken dialogue – is striking.

Masonic funeral music, K477

Opening with deep 'sighs' on the oboes, echoed by three basset-horns and double-bassoon, this is one of the most tragic and austere of Mozart's orchestral pieces. The use of a plainchant melody from the *Lamentations of Jeremiah* adds to the atmosphere of grief.

Duos for violin & viola, K423 & 424

These two miraculous pieces are the portal to the inner workings of chamber music. The two players are treated as equals virtually throughout, and Mozart's scoring for this slenderest of ensembles is endlessly inventive.

IN MOURNING:
The *Lamentations of Jeremiah*
add to the austerity of the
Masonic funeral music

8 String Quintet in G minor, K516

AT THE END of May 1787, Mozart's father dies. Just a few weeks earlier, Mozart completes his G minor String Quintet – the pinnacle of his chamber-music output. In a letter to his father, Mozart pens the much-quoted words: 'As death... is the true goal of our existence, I have formed during the last few years such close relations with this best and truest friend of mankind, that his image is no longer terrifying to me, but rather very soothing and consoling...'

The music transcends mere biographical context: at this time, after all, the debt-ridden Mozart is teaching and composing desperately for ready cash. But here, Mozart realises a depth of vision not seen or heard before. It seems to be in his quintets, rather than his quartets, that Mozart reaches this degree of transcendence. It's as though he's found the balance of instruments easier and more rewarding to handle: violin set against cello, with three-part harmony in the middle; violin against viola with string-trio accompaniment; and a high grouping against a low one – as so memorably in the opening of this G minor Quintet. There's a degree of urgent emotional engagement in the aspiring phrases and dying chromatic falls of the first movement, which points the way to the expressive palette of *Don Giovanni* – already brewing in mind and spirit. And the muted *Adagio*, with its distant modulation, certainly breathes the air of another planet.

STRING SENSATION:
The Met Chamber Ensemble performs Mozart's String Quintet in G minor

RECOMMENDED RECORDING

Philip Dukes (viola),
The Nash Ensemble
Hyperion
CDA67861/3

9 Clarinet Concerto in A, K622

THE CLARINET CONCERTO, Mozart's last instrumental work, and indeed his last complete work of any kind, figures here because it seems to be a true swansong, singing out the very heart and spirit of Mozart through the instrument closest to him. The Concerto is written for the virtuoso Anton Stadler, and is originally to have been a basset-horn concerto in G. But Mozart decides in favour of Stadler's basset-clarinet. This instrument's extra compass is exploited by Mozart, putting the clarinets' contrasting registers against each other, both to cunning technical and eloquently expressive effect. Cradled by flutes, bassoons and horns, this envoi, with its lovingly written slow movement, incarnates so much of the fully ripe sensibility of its composer. Mozart's treatment of the clarinet, and of the orchestral woodwind here, will never be surpassed: life for the clarinet won't be the same.

CLASSICAL INSTRUMENTS:
A copy of a basset-clarinet that was made for Anton Stadler

RECOMMENDED RECORDING

Fabio di Casola (clarinet);
Musikkollegium
Winterthur/Douglas Boyd
Sony 88697646722

GETTY, ALAMY

10 Requiem, K626

WHILE WORKING ON *The Magic Flute*, Mozart receives a commission from a stranger to compose a requiem, but under conditions of secrecy. Count von Walsegg wanted a requiem for his wife, to be played every year on her anniversary – and some have suggested he might have wanted to pass it off as his own work. With the encouragement of his own wife, Mozart accepted the challenge, and was paid a part-fee, with the rest to follow on completion. The deadline, according to one report, was four weeks. But Mozart had to go to Prague to conduct *Tito* – and the deadline continued to hang over him.

Mozart starts work, concentratedly, on 8 October 1791. And on 20 November, he takes to his bed with a worsening of the spells of ill health he had suffered during the last year. On 3 December, his condition appears to improve – and the next day a few close friends gather to sing over with him part of the still-unfinished Requiem. That evening, Mozart's illness worsens, and just before 1am on 5 December, he dies, aged 35 with an initial cause of death registered as 'severe military fever'.

At Mozart's death, only the Introitus of the Requiem is fully scored. All the other movements, from the Kyrie fugue to the end of the Hostias, are only sketched. Franz Xaver Süssmayr, who has written the recitatives for *La clemenza di Tito*, completes much of the Requiem.

The presence of an incomplete Requiem as Mozart's very last work delights scholars, commentators, playwrights and novelists to the present day. Again, the temptation to fuse life and work must be resisted: Mozart's last commission just happens to be for a requiem, after all. But on the day he died, Mozart himself declares: 'Didn't I say before that I was writing this Requiem for myself?' And, according to one eyewitness account, 'his last movement was an attempt to express with his mouth the drum passages in the Requiem.' On hearing of Mozart's death, Haydn says: 'Posterity will not see such a talent again in a hundred years!' And, as the American musicologist HC Robbins Landon later added, 'Posterity has not seen it in two hundred.' ∎

RECOMMENDED RECORDING

Dame Emma Kirkby, Carolyn Watkinson, Anthony Rolfe-Johnson & David Thomas; Chorus and Orchestra of The Academy of Ancient Music/ Christopher Hogwood **Decca 411 7122**

Growing up in public

Martin Hoyle weighs up how much of a role hindsight plays in our estimation of Mozart's early operas, and to what extent the works truly show evidence of a prodigious talent

I f, as Wordsworth maintained, the child is father to the man, there's a temptation to see the fully-fledged genius in everything that Mozart composed from infancy onwards. Mozart began his career as a prodigy and he died leaving unparalleled masterpieces. The tendency is to overlook the process in between. Of course, the child composer of *Apollo et Hyacinthus* showed astonishing melodic fluency and skill in harmony and orchestral texture – for an 11-year-old; and some exquisite movements for a composer of any age. But only hindsight would tint this Latin intermezzo for student performance with the humanity of *The Marriage of Figaro* or the heart-stopping depths of *Così fan tutte*. For the modern commentator the problem recurs: over-eagerness to spot the genius before the talent was actually adult.

If you're determined not to be influenced by the fact that this is Mozart, it is easy to miss the hint of characterisation that the boy shows in *Apollo* – Hyacinthus' aria about the gods nicely distinguishes between their benign and menacing moods. The story may be stilted, the emotional range limited, but there's a sense of drama already present, human feelings contrasted and compared.

Early promise

Apollo et Hyacinthus is Mozart's first staged work (1767), composed when he was 11 and conceived as an intermezzo during the play *Clementia Croesi* in the Benedictine School in Salzburg. A year later, the boy tackled the conventions of comic opera. *La finta semplice* (The pretend simpleton) was composed for Vienna but, as Mozart's indignant father has informed prosperity, production there was prevented by intrigues – notably, doubts were cast on the piece's authenticity as a child's work. It was provincial Salzburg, the Mozarts' hometown, that finally saw the premiere in 1769.

Mozart reacts to the Italian *buffo*, or comic, tradition with relish: he takes happily to the mixture of serious and comic in this typically intricate, artificial plot. There's patter for comedy and spacious aria for the deeper moment. The character of Rosina enjoys the widest range of depicted emotions – and, in the aria 'Senti l'eco', some of the most sheerly beautiful music. Above all, the convention of solo arias following one another is modified by long, concerted finales that portray mood swings and changing dramatic situations: an indication of great things to come.

Meanwhile, Dr Anton Mesmer's Viennese garden had provided the setting for ▶

GETTY

NEW INSTRUMENTS: Mozart sits at the harpsichord, which was popular in the mid-18th century. However, it would soon be eclipsed by the rise of the fortepiano

HARD AT WORK: The child prodigy is discovered composing by his father

a little *Singspiel* with traces of opera *comique* and pastoral lyricism. *Bastien und Bastienne* exudes charm, if no great dramatic impetus – perhaps inevitable in a work based on a French operatic parody of Rousseau's *Le devin du village*: amours, misunderstandings and mock wisdom dispensed by a comic sage. Germanic, simple, sweet, sometimes four-square, with a dash of what sounds like the unborn Beethoven, Mozart's *Singspiel* style was there, waiting for *Die Entführung as dem Serail* and, more eagerly, Papageno and his magic chimes in *Die Zauberflöte*.

First steps in opera seria

Despite its hints of Mozart's 'German' style, *Bastien* must have seemed a minor digression in the boy's operatic development by the time *Mitridate, re di Ponto* appeared triumphantly in Milan. At

the age of 14, the composer hurls himself into the world of *opera seria* – in its seriousness the opposite of *buffo* – with long, showy arias and its formulaic plot. At first hearing, the weaknesses are more apparent than the strengths: the arias are too long, predictable in shape, and sometimes too eagerly florid at the expense of character-painting.

Significantly, some of the original cast were less critical. The soprano who played Aspasia was delighted by the little Austrian's arias. But then Mozart worked on the arias after only meeting the singers concerned, even gratifying the tenor D'Ettore's insistence on a quota of high B flats and Cs. He also catered to the strengths of the orchestra – at almost 60 it was the largest he had dealt with – and provided a notable horn *obbligato* for Sifare's 'Lungi da te'. Sartorino, the

original castrato Sifare, also left a singer's verdict on his duet with Aspasia ('Se viver non degg'io'): if it wasn't a success, he averred, he'd be castrated again! Recent productions have brought out not only the opera's musical beauty but also the occasional emotional surge that adds a dramatic undertow to the score, even if the characters are not yet fully developed.

Mitridate was successful enough to prompt more Italian commissions for the 15-year-old musician, though *Ascanio in Alba* was perhaps not the ideal follow-up for a young composer with an instinct for the theatric and a feeling for human emotions. A '*festa teatrale*' for a royal marriage, the work is dominated by fine chorale writing and dances, and is hamstrung by the allegorical weight of its Virgil-inspired plot, memorable chiefly for identifying Venus with the Empress Maria Theresa and

BULL'S-EYE: Rehearsals of *Ascanio in Alba* at the Milan opera house

Hercules with the Duke Ercole d'Este – respective mother and father of the happy pair.

Finding his range

Earlier in the same year, Mozart had been preparing another ceremonial piece for performance. *Il sogno di Scipione* is a one-acter that was variously described as an 'azione teatrale' or a 'serenata', composed for the jubilee of the Archbishop of Salzburg, but the amiable Schrattenbach died before the performance date. The stately legend of Scipio Africanus's choice between the rival claims of Fortune and Constancy is not enlivened by vocal variety in the principals: three tenors, three sopranos. The work is most notable as Mozart's first professional acquaintance with the work of Metastasio, the most prolific and influential of neo-Classical librettists, to whose work he would return. It was eventually performed to celebrate the enthronement of the new archbishop, Colloredo, generally considered to be the unsympathetic and bullying employer who drove Mozart from Salzburg.

Though Mozart's annual operatic commissions for Milan seemed established, his third, *Lucio Silla*, proved the last work he would write for Italy. Was it a portent that the first performance was delayed by two hours as the Emperor wrote letters? By now, nearly 17, the composer was

Nearly 17, Mozart was champing at the bit to set real feelings to music, to illuminate real tensions between real people

almost audibly champing at the bit to set real feelings to music, to illuminate real tensions between real people. *Silla* marks extraordinary progress in the depiction of heartfelt emotions – love, fear, foreboding, and determination – by both vocal and orchestral means.

Again, the young composer tailored the vocal writing to his singers' specialities. In the case of the title role this was a mixed blessing, since the relatively obscure tenor was, at best, adequate; *Silla*'s music goes through the formal motions but little ▶

COMIC OPERA: Preparations for a performance of *La finta semplice* at the Ekhof Theatre, Germany – one of the oldest stages in the world

else. The pallid portrait is all the more noticeable compared with the vividness of Cecilo (created by the castrato Rauzzini) and, above all, the embattled Giunia. This defiant heroine anticipates Constanze in *Die Entführung* in personality and looks forward to *Don Giovanni*'s Donna Anna in forceful musical depiction. The virtuoso coloratura ('Ah, se il crudel periglio') that depicts her horror as she imagines her beloved dead ('Fra i pensier piu funesti') puts the role on a par with Vitallia in *Tito*. Grief alternates with scornful pride ('Della sponda tenebrosa') and the sombre mausoleum lament of 'O del padre ombra diletta' adds another, tender dimension.

Mozart in the buffo

Cecilo's music displays the wide-leaping intervals that Rauzzini demanded, those swoops between high and low and back again that Mozart later notably used for Fiordiligi's protestations of fidelity in 'Come scoglio' in *Così* – and elsewhere to indicate

instability. But what intrigues above all in Silla's score is the use of the orchestra, especially in accompanied recitative. For the first time, Mozart revels in wreathing the stately utterances of pre-romanticism with textual and harmonial richness – again, it's not mere hindsight to observe how much of the orchestral writing looks ahead not only to *Idomeneo*, but to the darker colours of *Don Giovanni*.

Are we in danger of reading too much into an early work simply because it's by Mozart?

Again, are we in danger of reading too much into an early work simply because it's by Mozart? I think not; it's impossible to hail his next opera, *La finta giadiniera* (The pretend gardener), as anything more than a distant pointer to *Figaro*. This *dramma giocoso* premiered in the carnival season

at Munich in early 1775, shortly before Mozart's 19th birthday. After the two-year gap since *Silla*, the composer seems to feel his way into *opera buffa*, as if rusty in the genre he had tackled only with *La finta semplice* at the age of 12. It's fascinating to see Mozart hampered by a weak libretto; the plot's mix of artificial and sentimental, serious and comic (and mad scenes that one is uncertain whether or not to take seriously), marks vacillation rather than blend.

Strengths include the Act II finale – nearly half an hour of music reflecting the drama's twists and turns, anticipating the great Act II finale of *Figaro* – and sharp comic characterisations that foreshadow later works. The piece never entirely caught on, though a German *Singspiel* version was already doing the rounds in Mozart's lifetime.

Presaging the Romantics

Three months later, *Il re pastore* was performed for a Habsburg archducal visit ▶

STARRING ROLE: A 1994 performance of *Lucio Silla* in Salzburg, Austria

to Salzburg, where a 19-year-old Mozart was becoming ever more disenchanted with his servile position in the Archbishop's employment. This 'serenata' setting of classical legend, with its wealth of allusion to the ruling dynasty, was a glorified masque with little stage action or effects. The score is memorable chiefly for its exquisite orchestration and the limpid melodic qualities of certain arias, the most famous being 'L'amero, saro costante' with its violin *obbligato*.

If *Il re pastore* scarcely qualifies as opera, Mozart's next stage score lays claim to nothing more than incidental music for a play. For a modern listener, the chief interest of *Thamos, Konig in Agypten*, written by Tobias von Gebler, lies in anticipation of *Die Zauberflöte*. The Ancient Egyptian setting and solemn moral certainties, benign high priest (the heroine's father in disguise) and wicked high priestess, look forward to at least one side of Mozart's last opera. Choruses, solos and orchestral interludes provide a mixed bag, since Mozart frequently revised and added to the score. Much influenced by

Georg Benda's gift for melodrama – in the original sense, spoken drama accompanied by music – Mozart makes the orchestra comment vibrantly on the action with an emotional vitality that almost merits the term 'melodrama' in its modern usage, and anticipates the Romantics. The moods run the gamut from the hero's nobility to the traitor's anguished death. *Thamos* was staged in April 1774 in Vienna. In sporadic revisions and additions over the next four years, Mozart's musico-dramatic development can be traced, from the monumental to the passionate, and the relaxed mastery of some of the choral writing, including the most melodically catchy stage prayer until Rossini's *Moses*.

First fruit of greatness

Melody is what one remembers from *Zaide* – the *Singspiel* that Mozart left tantalizingly unfinished in 1780. The previous three years had been marked by Mozart's passionate longing to write more opera – it's extraordinary to note the five opera-less years since *La finta giardiniera* (*Il re pastore* hardly counts). *Zaide* was

composed partly in response to the Emperor's enthusiasm for a national German school. The story of lovers escaping from a Turkish harem anticipates *Die Entführung* (its original title was *Die Serial*), but it still uses melodrama, where the later work favours a recitative form. Like *Thamos*, *Zaide* incorporates what Mozart had learned in his wanderings from Munich to Paris via Mannheim, most notably in orchestral richness and exquisitely judged instrumentation. Combined with a lovely vocal line, these qualities makes *Zaide's* 'Ruhe sanft' (Slumber aria) one of the gems of his early operas. Since its first staging in 1866, attempts have been made to complete the work – one version, written by Italo Svevo, played at the Old Vic in London in the 1970s – none of them satisfactory (especially as in the original the lovers are revealed as brother and sister). Yet *Zaide* contains moments of real operatic talent – from a rondo about a caged nightingale to the dramatic quartet, where love, lamentation and vengeful vindictiveness intermingle. And that has nothing to do with hindsight. ■

UNFINISHED WORK: The uncompleted opera *Zaide* performed by the City of Birmingham Touring Opera

ALAMY X2

A genius at 20

Erik Levi looks at the 20-year-old Mozart's non-operatic works – does he find a fully-fledged composer, or one who's still only getting started?

IF MOZART HAD been struck by a thunderbolt at the age of 20, how might we have regarded him today?

Perhaps the most remarkable thing would be the sheer volume of music that Mozart had written – over 250 works from almost every genre. A workaholic, he rarely rested on his laurels and always sought out new opportunities and challenges. Nevertheless, despite attaining astounding fluency in so many types of music at such an early age, the teenage composer probably didn't produce anything as perfectly formed and totally original as the 17-year-old Mendelssohn in his overture to *A Midsummer Night's Dream*.

Of course, we should not discount his achievements up to 1776. There is already ample evidence of an extraordinary musical mind at work. He ingested many influences of the day, in particular the style of Johann Christian Bach, whom he first encountered at the age of eight in London. Despite his youth, Mozart absorbed and transformed these stylistic traits, as any great creative artist would. The huge number of symphonies (possibly as many as 43) that he had written since penning his first in London demonstrates great confidence in the medium. And there are already glimpses of something far more individual, particularly in some of the slow movements. One of the earliest examples comes from the 12-year-old composer's Symphony No. 6 in F, K43, where Mozart writes a delicate instrumental aria.

> *A workaholic, Mozart rarely rested on his laurels and always sought out new opportunities and challenges*

The teenage years

By the time Mozart composed the Symphony in G minor, K183, and the Symphony in A, K201 – in 1773 and 1774 respectively – he could already have been regarded as a seasoned veteran of the genre. But it's only in these two contrasting works – the first filled with bold and dramatic gestures reminiscent of *Sturm und Drang* and the second, combining chamber-music-like intimacy with theatrical impulsiveness – that a truly personal voice is fully developed.

In contrast to his huge symphonic output, Mozart proceeded cautiously with concertos. In his earliest attempts, he set himself an unusual challenge by utilising pre-existing solo sonata movements (composed by CPE Bach and Schobert among others) and adapting and extending them with different contexts. Its practical purpose was to allow Mozart to grapple with the sonata's particular structural problems.

Even after completing four such works, he seemed reluctant to write any unique concertos. In fact, five years later, he completed another trio of concertos, K107, based on the keyboard sonatas of JC Bach. Only after this did he compose a completely original work – his first fully-fledged keyboard Concerto in D, K175, from 1773. After its success Mozart quickly attempted other concertante works, the Concertone in C for two violins and orchestra, K190, which includes solos for oboe and cello, and the Bassoon Concerto, K191, which demonstrates an instinctive understanding of wind instruments. Surpassing these were three concertos he composed for violin (K216 in G, K218 in D and K219 in A), which were completed astonishingly fast, during the autumn of 1775.

Taken as a whole, Mozart's achievements during 1776 were not quite as prodigious as those in the previous year. Personal circumstances may have had some bearing on this, as he had been stuck in Salzburg since March 1775. Having enjoyed acclaim in courts throughout Europe as a child and teenager, it's easy to understand Mozart's frustrations.

A lack of motivation

As a result of his frustrations, Mozart's productivity dipped in his 20th year. He wrote no symphonies or stage works and focused his energies on entertainment music, especially compositions for wealthy patrons. Of these, the most ambitious is the Serenade in D, K250. Its elaborate design combines symphonic elements with concerto movements, featuring a solo violin.

Mozart spent much of 1776 composing church music, yet to what extent he enjoyed these works remains unanswered, for it seems odd that he should have written three masses, K257-59, all in the key of C. However one or two sacred works are interesting. The *Litaniae de venerabili altaris sacremento*, K243, from March 1776, for instance, is largely rather conventional, but it is a thrilling piece thanks to its dark movements and dramatic moments. The short *Veniti, populi*, K260, is also fascinating, as the composer exploits elaborate contrapuntal effects.

It should be mentioned that Mozart's Concerto in B flat, K238, for keyboard and orchestra, which he composed in January 1776, does contradict the idea that he was just killing time in his 20th year. This Concerto – which he wrote for himself – demonstrates a much more sophisticated approach to the musical dialogue between soloist and orchestra than its predecessor. In the outer movements the soloist exchanges witty pleasantries with the orchestra, while in the captivating slow movement, their relationship is subtler – the orchestra seems to galvanise the soloist, to create an increasingly elaborate and intense musical line.

While noting that the best of Mozart's work was still to emerge – especially after he made the move to Vienna in the 1780s – to quantify his life up to this point we can surely acknowledge his extraordinary talent.

MODERN PERFORMANCES

IDOMENEO

Semper Opera, Germany, 2012. Dir. Michael Schulz

Idomeneo **is based on the Greek myth of King Idomeneus. Idomeneo nearly drowns in a storm but is spared when he promises to kill the first man he sees. However, this turns out to be his son...**

PA IMAGES

Intimate letters

Pianist Dame Mitsuko Uchida feels closer to Mozart after reading a modern translation of his correspondence. Dirty words and all, it's an invaluable insight, she tells **Fiona Maddocks** in an interview from 2001

Scholarship and performance should go hand in hand. With the possible exception of early music, they rarely do. Dame Mitsuko Uchida, among the most inquisitive and striving of concert pianists, claims to have no time to keep up with the minutiae of academic discovery. If you express surprise at this admission, thinking that of all musicians she stands out for her cultivated and high-minded approach to her art, she shrieks with one of her famously explosive laughs. 'No way, no way! There are not enough hours in a day to follow the latest theories and discoveries of one scholar about one composer, let alone all those one plays! For that I would have to be a full-time academic and do nothing but read, or maybe teach a little. It's just not possible. I am a piano player!'

A fresh translation

Yet her life, she says, has been dramatically transformed by one man: Robert Spaethling. His translation of Mozart's letters, published in 2000 to great acclaim, has enhanced her understanding of a composer with whom she was long been on intimate terms. Her association with his music is long and deep. In 1982, she launched her British career with a complete cycle of Mozart's sonatas in London (where this Japanese concert pianist has since made her home). Soon after, she directed all the piano concertos from the keyboard and had her own television series in which she displayed her dazzling knowledge of both the man and his works. The bond is as strong as ever. So, could his letters really hold anymore surprises for her?

'I've read them before, of course, in many forms and guises, and skipped many, I'm sure. I've even staggered through them – and what a labour that was – in German. My German is good because I lived in Vienna for a time as a child, but Mozart's wild spelling, his grammar – it's impossible! The translation Spaethling has done is quite stunning. It makes real sense about Mozart and I think we ought to be grateful to him for doing this mammoth task. Not only are the letters very, very well translated but the book also gives you the structure of his life, and that is really difficult. He has chosen the best and annotated them brilliantly. You have to be a maniac like me, or a serious musician, to buy the complete letters in German, and to read all his sister Nannerl's boring diaries and so on. Even if you're truly obsessed, you start missing bits out. But this book is compulsive reading from start to finish.'

> ## MOZART'S WILD SPELLING, HIS GRAMMAR – IT'S IMPOSSIBLE! THE SPAETHLING TRANSLATION IS STUNNING

DECCA/MARCO BORGGREVE

A scholarly excess of good intentions, good manners and good taste has befuddled the publication of Mozart's letters, in German as well as in English. The fact is, Mozart loved talking dirty. His letters overflow with obscenities, bawdiness and smut in several different languages. There is no bodily function he is not happy to describe, even when writing to his mother. In a letter of 1777 to his father, Leopold, he adds a postscript, without apology and with rare understatement: 'My pen is coarse, I am not polite'. Translators and editors, however, have been timid in the face of such extravagant ribaldry, and set about cleaning, improving and disinfecting in order, one suspects, to protect the composer's spotless image and the reader's unsullied mind in equal measure.

Censoring the composer

Emily Anderson's classic translation, 'The Letters of Mozart and His Family' has been an invaluable reference since it was first published in 1938 but it, too, has a tendency to improve on Mozart's original language. In contrast, Spaethling, who has translated 275 letters (about two thirds of the correspondence) writes that his aim has been to 'bring out Mozart's own voice and diction by looking for close and suitable equivalents or approximations for his down-to-earth German vocabulary, the conversational structures of his sentences and even his phonetic spelling.' He also honours Mozart's exuberant departures into Italian, French and Latin, often mid-sentence. Indeed, the letters dart from fizzing humour to profound solemnity, from woeful money concerns to excited descriptions of lavish new items of clothing, as if Mozart himself were reading them aloud, so vividly do they dance off the page.

'The great thing about Mozart's letters is the element of fun, of wit, of intelligence. Germans themselves have not always wanted their great cultural hero to be seen making rhymes out of four-letter words or making scatological utterances.' says Uchida. 'It's as if

LEOPOLD MOZART: The majority of Mozart's correspondence was to his father

> SOME LETTERS ARE SERIOUS, SOME JUST AN EXCHANGE OF INFORMATION. BUT OTHERS ARE PURE PLAY

they're ashamed that this genius could do such a thing. Eventually in the late 1960s and early 1970s, the complete German edition came out and I don't suppose they worry about such things now. But Anderson's translation was fairly daring and for a while England was ahead in letting the letters speak for themselves. But not at all to the extent they do now, thanks to Spaethling. I don't know exactly what the cultural background of Mozart's time would have allowed, or whether these extraordinary and filthy word plays and games he so loves would just have been kept within the family. But he extends this wild style to all his correspondents. Maria Anna, his mother, even wrote to her husband in the same terms, so it was obviously common practice.'

The personal touch

Uchida's particular fascination is the way in which his letters in some ways mirror his style of composition. 'Ah – isn't it a blessing that we have them? It's amazing. He is so genial, such a warm

character, with such fascinating insights into human life. They give you so much to think about because he was such a lively linguist. Just as he wrote music, so he wrote letters and used words. And he gets quickly bored, and moves on to the next thing. It is all part of understanding him. Some of them are serious, some just an exchange of information. But others are pure play, from start to finish. They give you the whole sense of his life, and a picture of the music he was writing, and how those pieces happened and how they fitted in. The letters he wrote on the night of his mother's death are quite extraordinary. In effect he lied to Leopold, writing with the corpse next to him but telling his father she was merely ill, to spare him the shock and prepare him. In fact, for me the most fascinating time of his life was that trip to Paris (1778-79) because so many important events happened to him. That was his real growing up period. He began to free himself from his father Leopold, he falls in love, then his mother dies – how much more can you experience?'

One of Mozart's constant topics of conversation is the logistical headache of getting letters from one place to another – a week or two on average, if you were lucky. The many exchanges between Wolfgang and Leopold, in which the stern father quizzes about work and money, become increasingly strained as the correspondence grows more protracted. Questions asked with urgency might receive no reply for nearly a month.

After one particularly heated dispatch from his father, Mozart realises his last two letters had not reached their destination. On another occasion, he worries that one of the servants pocketed the

INSTRUMENTAL WORKS

Piano Sonatas
Dame Mitsuko Uchida (piano)
Philips 468 3562
Mozart's 18 Piano Sonatas may not pound the senses to quite the extent that Beethoven's do, but they're not exactly short of emotional intensity either. For interpretations that get to the very core of that emotional soul, few can match the complete recordings made by the brilliant Dame Mitsuko Uchida.

Organ works
Peter King (organ)
Regent REGCD244
It is all too easy to overlook that Mozart also composed some delightful works for the organ. Many appear on compilations featuring music by other composers, but for an all-Mozart programme, Peter King's engaging recital on the Bath Abbey organ is as good a place as any to begin.

ORCHESTRAL WORKS

Symphonies Nos 38-41
Scottish Chamber Orchestra/ Sir Charles Mackerras
Linn CKD 308
Sir Charles Mackerras's fresh and revelatory performances of Mozart's four last Symphonies set a new benchmark. The Scottish Chamber Orchestra is on top form, creating an exhilarating recording.

Piano Concertos
Daniel Barenboim (piano); English Chamber Orchestra
EMI 572 9302 (10 CDs)
From exuberant *allegros* to heartfelt *adagios*, Mozart's Piano Concertos come to vivid life in these classic performances from the English Chamber Orchestra and Daniel Barenboim.

Violin Concertos
Giuliano Carmignola (violin); Orchestra Mozart/ Claudio Abbado *DG 477 7371*
Packed with energy, charm and lyricism, these finely-turned performances cast Mozart's five Violin Concertos in fresh light. Giuliano Carmignola is alert to every detail, his tone bright and clean.

Horn Concertos
Dennis Brain (horn); Philharmonia/Herbert von Karajan *EMI 965 9362*
Horn player Dennis Brain takes centre stage in this effortlessly graceful 1953 recording. Brain brought these concertos some long-overdue recognition through his revelatory interpretation.

Flute Concertos/Flute and Harp Concerto
Emmanuel Pahud (flute), Marie-Pierre Langlamet (harp); Berlin Philharmonic/Claudio Abbado
EMI 085 1952
Flautist Emmanuel Pahud is on superlative form in this recording from 1997 of what must rank as some of Mozart's most sublime music.

CHAMBER MUSIC

String Quartets
The Amadeus Quartet
Deutsche Grammophon 477 8680
As full of variety as they are deftly crafted, Mozart's 23 Quartets include the famous 'Hunt' and 'Dissonance' Quartets. They were superbly recorded by the great Amadeus Quartet in the late-1960s.

Violin Sonatas
Itzhak Perlman (violin), Daniel Barenboim (piano)
Deutsche Grammophon 463 7492
In Mozart's 36 Violin Sonatas, the violin and piano have a largely equal role. Therefore, a close musical partnership, such as that between Itzhak Perlman and Daniel Barenboim, is a must.

Clarinet Quintet
Dame Thea King (basset-clarinet); Gabrieli String Quartet *Hyperion CDA 66199*
Written by Mozart for the virtuoso clarinettist Anton Stadler, the Clarinet Quintet is a sublime showcase for the instrument. In this recording, clarinettist Dame Thea King, brings out the music's beauty.

**Serenade No. 13 in G,
'Eine kleine Nachtmusik'**
Academy of St Martin in the Fields/Sir Neville Marriner
Australian Eloquence 480 4722
The catchy opening has become (over) familiar from on-hold music, but for a performance that reveals its joyous gusto and sparkle, turn to this classic 1970 recording.

Serenade for winds in B flat major, 'Gran partita'
Albion Ensemble *Helios CDH55093*
Composed for two oboes, two clarinets, two basset horns, two bassoons, four horns and a double bass, a successful performance requires a perfect balance between all. The Albion Ensemble achieves just that.

MULTIPLE GUISES: Da Ponte
lived a long and varied life,
from impoverished Jew to
philandering Catholic

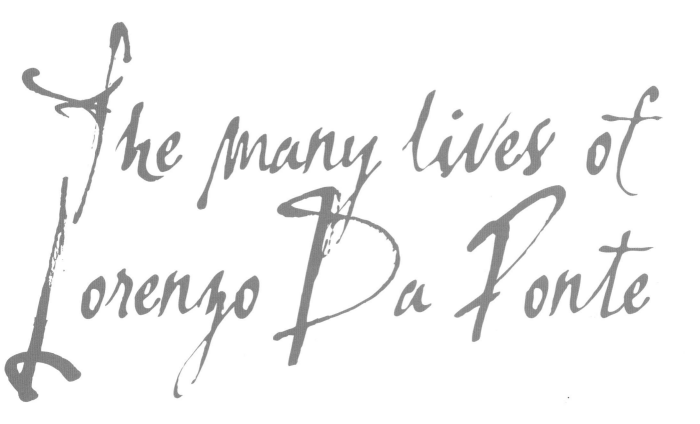

The many lives of Lorenzo Da Ponte

Working with Mozart and counting Casanova as a close friend, librettist Lorenzo Da Ponte lived an extraordinary life. Anthony Holden profiles the man who wrote the words to some of the greatest operas

From 18th century Vienna to 19th century America: the life of Lorenzo Da Ponte, librettist of three of Mozart's greatest operas – *The Marriage of Figaro, Don Giovanni* and *Così fan tutti* – begins in Venice and hurtles across Europe before winding up in New York, where he lies buried beneath the flight-path into JFK Airport.

Born in 1749, in the small Venetian hill-town of Ceneda (now Vittorio Veneto), his real name was Emanuele Conegliano, the eldest of three sons to a Jewish tanner. Uneducated and illiterate, he ran wild until he was 14 years old, when his widowed father fell in love with a 16-year-old Christian girl. In order for him to marry her, the Jewish family had to be received into the Catholic church. It was the custom at the time for the eldest son to assume the name of the bishop who baptised them. Therefore, Emanuele Conegliano became Lorenzo Da Ponte.

AFTER NUMEROUS AFFAIRS, NOT LEAST WITH MARRIED WOMEN, DA PONTE WAS BANISHED FROM VENICE

With Bishop Da Ponte as their sponsor, the three sons' fortunes took a turn for the better. Lorenzo Da Ponte received a classical education, began to write poetry, and became a Catholic priest (Abbé). Appointed a professor, he soon became disenchanted with academia and when he was just 24 years old, he resigned to seek a new life in 'the permanent fancy-dress ball that was Venice'.

The once mighty imperial Venice was then partying its way towards becoming merely the most beautiful city on Earth. As the French Revolution loomed, Casanova, the prototype libertine, was making his mark on the city and would shortly become Da Ponte's friend. But first the Abbé had to make some conquests of his own.

After numerous affairs, not least with married women, the poet-priest was banished from Venice. Wandering west across Europe, he arrived in Vienna in 1781 with a letter of introduction to the ▶

KING OF GERMANY: Emperor Joseph II was a great patron of the arts, and known as the 'Musical King'

Sig.ra *Andriana Ferrarese, Principal Sing* at the *King's Theater*.

Tho' sweeter notes than *Philomela's Lay*;
Melt on her Lips, and snatch the sense away;
Yet 'midst these sounds, new Pleasures are in store,
We on the Singer th'Actress now adore. **LR**

LEADING LADY: An engraving of Adriana Del Bene, Da Ponte's mistress

court composer, Antonio Salieri, who persuaded Emperor Joseph II to appoint Da Ponte as his theatre-poet. Soon he made his name writing librettos for Salieri and other leading composers.

Meeting with Mozart

It was in 1873 that Da Ponte met the young and unemployed composer from Salzburg. Mozart was thrilled to befriend the Abbé, six years his senior. 'We have a new poet here, Abbé Da Ponte', he wrote excitedly to his father who was in Salzburg.

In the wake of *Die Entführung aus dem Serail*, Mozart yearned to abandon the German tradition for Italian opera. 'In opera, the poetry must be the obedient daughter of the music,' he wrote. 'The best thing is when a good composer, who understands the stage enough to make sound suggestions, meets an able poet, that true phoenix.'

Mozart had met his 'true phoenix' in Da Ponte, whose poetic skill and theatrical instincts made an indispensable contribution to the three masterpieces they would now write together. Without his 'able poet', Mozart might not have reached the full heights of which he was capable, in the genre that meant most to him. On the face

'THE BEST THINK IS WHEN A GOOD COMPOSER MEETS AN ABLE POET, THAT TRUE PHOENIX.' MOZART

of it, the pair were ill-matched; Mozart had worked his entire life, whereas for Da Ponte life was for enjoying.

The Italian composer Paisiello had recently enjoyed a huge success with an opera of Beaumarchais's play, *The Barber of Seville*. Now Mozart persuaded Da Ponte to make a libretto from its scandalous sequel, *The Marriage of Figaro*. The Emperor had banned the play as 'subversive', so they were forced to work in secret.

By November 1785, Da Ponte had delivered a draft to Mozart, who wrote the music in six weeks. Not until then did the Court Poet inform the Emperor what he and Mozart had been up to. When Joseph II reminded his poet that the play was banned, Da Ponte assured him that the process of converting it into an opera had obliged him to shorten the piece – omitting those scenes that might offend. 'As for the music,' he added, 'it is remarkably beautiful.' Once the Emperor had discovered this for himself, he sanctioned *Figaro* for performance.

It was with this work that opera would come of age. When Da Ponte was born, Handel reigned supreme; four years after his death, Wagner would make his debut. Da Ponte and Mozart were the twin pillars of that transition, transforming opera into an art form exploring human issues in an accessible, realistic manner, via characters the audience could recognise, and with whom they could identify.

Mixed reception

With different characters of whatever social status sharing views and aspirations, *opera buffa* reflected the Enlightenment ideal of the similarity of all mankind, regardless of birth or rank. As yet, however, it was regarded as an inferior form to *seria*. This was soon to be shown up as mere snobbery. But *Figaro* enjoyed only nine performances in Vienna before being dropped from the repertoire. In Prague, it proved such a triumph that Mozart was commissioned to write another opera, for which Da Ponte suggested a reworking of the old Don Juan legend. As he set to work on *Don Giovanni* for Mozart, Da Ponte was also writing librettos for Salieri and Martin. 'You won't succeed!' laughed the Emperor. Nonetheless, two months later, Da Ponte delivered his manuscript to Mozart, who set it to music in time for a triumphant premiere on 29 October 1787.

Again, the piece failed in Vienna and at the end of the 1788 season the Emperor closed down the opera as he considered it costly and inappropriate while the nation was at war with the Turks. Faced with ruin, Da Ponte hatched a plan to keep it going at no cost to the Emperor – who himself commissioned their third collaboration, *Così Fan Tutte*, one of only two original works among Da Ponte's 50-plus librettos (and the only Mozart opera commissioned in Vienna). The role of Fiordiligi was written for his latest mistress, a singer called Adriana del Bene, better-known as La Ferrarese.

Joseph II never saw his brainchild. By its first night, he already lay dying. As Da Ponte composed an ode in his memory, jealous enemies at court were busy persuading the new emperor, Leopold II, that his poet had been plotting against him. Soon he found himself forbidden entry to the Imperial Theatre to see one of his own operas. Within days, as he had been from Venice ten years before, Da Ponte was banished from Vienna.

Kicking his heels in Trieste, he met a beautiful English-born girl named Nancy Grahl, whom he promptly married – to the astonishment of all who knew him. Via a visit to his friend Casanova in Bohemia, the couple headed for Paris. In Da Ponte's pocket was a letter of introduction to Marie-Antoinette from her late brother, Joseph.

The American chapter

Casanova saw Da Ponte off with some memorable advice: 'Don't go to Paris, go to London. Once there, never visit the Café degl'Italiani, and never sign your name.' When Da Ponte heard of Marie-Antoinette's imprisonment, he took Casanova's advice – and headed for London.

Here, for the next decade, he was poet at the King's Theatre, Haymarket, then dedicated to Italian opera. But the gullible Da Ponte fell foul of the theatre's roguish manager, William Taylor, ignoring Casanova's advice by signing his name to some business documents. As the scale of Taylor's mismanagement became clear, Da Ponte was arrested and imprisoned 30 times in three months.

Unable to support his wife and children, he put them on a boat to America, where Nancy had relatives. After nine more wretched months in London, he was warned that he again faced arrest for debt. This time Da Ponte decided to run for it. He did a midnight flit to Gravesend, where he boarded the packet *Columbia* for Philadelphia, arriving in June 1805, with only a violin. What little

money he had left, he gambled away on the voyage. The rest of his life – another *vita nuova*, lasting more than 30 years – would be spent in the young United States. After a false start as a grocer, Da Ponte found work as a teacher of Italian, founding the Manhattan Academy for Young Gentlemen. Prospering at last, he made it his personal mission to infuse the New World with a love and knowledge of Italian culture, particularly music and literature. After a diversion to Pennsylvania, where he ran a millinery and a distillery, he returned to New York to become the first professor of Italian in the US, at Columbia College (now University), in 1825.

Running a bookshop on the side, Da Ponte presented Columbia and the New York Public Library with volumes of Italian literature, which form the nucleus of their collections to this day. In 1828, as he neared 80, he brought the first Italian opera company to America, not least for a performance of *Don Giovanni*. In his last decade, he built and ran America's first opera house.

A lifelong legacy

Da Ponte died on 17 August 1838, five months before his 90th birthday. He had proved an archetype of the ideal American immigrant, contributing as much to his adopted homeland as it had offered him – which is probably how he would like to be remembered. But his name will live on, perhaps to his own surprise, as that of Mozart's librettist. ∎

GRAND ENTRANCE: The front of the King's Theatre in Haymarket before it was destroyed by fire in 1789

15 UNUSUAL USES FOR MOZART

Does Mozart's music really help brain development? Jeremy Pound
uncovers some alternative uses of the great man's works

S o, as he sat down to put pen to score, what did Mozart think his music might achieve? Something on the lines of pleasing listeners, challenging performers, satisfying patrons and keeping the wolf from his own door, we suspect. Think again, Wolfgang – you've underestimated yourself. Undisputed genius though he was, he can surely have had little idea how, two centuries later, masterpieces such as *Eine kleine Nachtmusik* and *The Magic Flute* would be credited with powers stretching well beyond the concert hall and opera house. It was Alfred A Tomatis who, in 1991, suggested that listening to the great man's music helped brain development. Suddenly, inquisitive scientists, innovative farmers, ingenious marketeers and the like were looking at just what the great Austrian could do for them. Here, we present 15 of the finest examples of how Mozart has been put to use...

1. More alcoholic wine
Carlo Cignozzi, a wine-marker, plays *The Magic Flute* into his Brunello vineyard – the grapes ripen in 14 days as opposed to the normal 20, which apparently increases the wine's alcoholic content.

2. Less alcoholic students
In 1999, officials at Pittsburgh University got so fed up with its students rolling around paralytic that they decided to play *Eine kleine Nachtmusik* on campus between 10pm and 2am in the hope that it would discourage drunken behaviour.

3. Clearer water
Masaru Emoto, an entrepreneur and doctor of alternative medicine, has apparently proved that water that has had Mozart played to it produces clearer crystals when frozen than water that has been exposed to rock music. We are not making any of this up.

4. More plentiful milk
In 2007, Spanish dairy farmer Hans Pieter Sieber discovered the power of the composer's Concerto for Flute and Harp on his heifers. He played the work to his cows as they lined up for milking, and it brought a general air of bovine calm and contentment, which equated in real terms to an increased production of milk of up to six litres per animal.

5. Eggier eggs
The organisers of the 2003 Mannheim Mozart Festival thought it would be fun to play 14 days solid of Mozart to 3,000 hens at a local farm. While the quantity of eggs did not increase, when served the Mozartian eggs at the festival, concertgoers said they 'definitely tasted better'. Possibly not the most scientific study ever.

6. Calmer dogs
In 2006, an RSPCA centre in Somerset unleashed a pack of 'Woofgang Amadeus' puns when it revealed that it had installed a sound system to help out when some of its canine residents were getting a little feisty. The dogs would quickly relax to Mozart and Bach, but not so to pop or dance music.

7. Friskier sharks
In 2007, scientists at the Blackpool Sea Life Centre played Bloodnose, a 20-year-old male brown shark, the Romanza from *Eine kleine Nachtmusik* to try and get him to show a little interest in 15-year-old Lucy. Sadly, the experiment was not successful.

8. Smarter rodents
In 1998, cellist-turned-experimental-psychologist Frances Rauscher played Mozart's Sonata in D Major for Two Pianos to her lab rats, and discovered that they could negotiate a labyrinth faster than under silent conditions. Similar results have been shown with mice, who also attacked each other when exposed to rock music.

9. Sportier athletes
Mozart can speed up people, too. In April 2004, Dr Thanassis Dritsas, advisor to the Greek Olympic team, incorporated 15

minutes of Mozart to the start of the athletes' training. Four months later, Greece won six gold medals, its biggest haul since 1896.

10. Fewer yobs
In the early 2000's, Tyne and Wear Metro successfully put off unruly types from loitering around its station with occasional blasts of Mozart and Vivaldi. 'They seem to loathe it,' said a delighted spokesman. Which is all a bit depressing, really.

11. Quicker growing babies
Playing Mozart to premature babies can make them grow faster. The reason, doctors say, is because babies use less energy when listening to the composer's music, and so put on more weight more quickly. But it has to be Mozart. 'The repetitive melodies in Mozart's music may be affecting the organisational centres of the brain's cortex,' says Dr Dror Mandel.

12. …and quicker growing fish
An acceleration in growth was observed when bream at the Agricultural University of Athens were played the Romanza from *Eine kleine Nachtmusik* for the first 89 days of their lives. Given that a date with a dinner plate awaited them, one imagines that the fish were none too chuffed about this speeding up of matters…

13. Tastier ham
Likewise, pigs at the Embutidos Fermin meat company in La Alberca, Spain, are treated to Mozart to make them tastier. The night before they meet their maker, they are lulled to sleep with Mozart. This soothes and calms the animals. If they're scared they produce epinephrine. But when calmed by Mozart, the meat is delicious.

14. More breakdownable sewage
A German sewage centre has recorded a noticeable acceleration in the breakdown of biomass since it started playing *The Magic Flute* throughout the plant – so much so that the centre saves around 1,000 euros a month. 'We think the secret is in the vibrations,' the chief operator explained. 'But you need the right frequencies and the right music, and Mozart hits the spot.'

15. Sillier biologists
In 2001, researchers at Trinity University, Texas, showed that plants photosynthesise more quickly when 'listening' to the Concerto in G, than to Bach, or in silence. Or did they? While the research paper seems complete with figures and long words that non-biologists don't understand, the citing of the nebulous 'Concerto in G' raises suspicions that are confirmed with likes of B Spears and WJ Clinton listed in the sources at the end. Ho ho. Those wacky lab researchers. ■

An anniversary to forget

The Nazis celebrated the 150th anniversary of Mozart's death in style. However, at the hands of propagandists, the composer and his works were given a new apparel, as **Erik Levi** discovers

Given the dire events that affected Germany at the end of 1941, it seems rather extraordinary that Mozart should even have registered on the consciousness of the Nazis. During this period, divisions of the German army were literally freezing to death on the Eastern front, while experiencing the bitter hardships of the Russian winter. Furthermore, the Soviets proved to be a far more potent adversary than expected, launching a number of offensives that would cost the Germans even more lives.

And yet these setbacks were deliberately kept concealed from the German public. Instead, the Nazis instigated a meticulously choreographed 'feel-good-factor' propaganda drive to try and reassure the nation that it was still on course for the ultimate victory. Using any means at their disposal, the regime's spin-doctors were anxious to maintain a sense of patriotism, as well as deflect attention away from the harsh realities of war. It was therefore no accident that they should alight on Mozart to spearhead their campaign, particularly since the 150th anniversary of his death happened to take place during that year. Such a momentous event in the musical calendar supplied the regime with the cynical justification for launching an unprecedented number of celebrations in the composer's memory.

The appropriation of Mozart as a Nazi icon calls for some comment, especially as many people still assume that Wagner and Bruckner, and to a lesser extent Beethoven, were the regime's exclusive musical gods. Yet after Hitler's annexation of Austria in 1938, the Nazis were able to claim Mozart ▶

> During this period, divisions of the German army were freezing to death on the Eastern front

THE NAZI INFLUENCE: Hitler sits with German ministers in the governmental balcony at the German Opera house

as one of their own – a profoundly 'German' (rather than Austrian) figure whose achievement, they argued, foreshadowed the great 19th century Romantics. To repackage the composer in such terms required a good deal of manipulation of historical information – something to which the Nazis were no strangers. For example, it was simply unacceptable to concur with the great philosopher Friedrich Nietzsche, who said that Mozart was 'the last great European' – a composer who was equally responsive to musical styles from a variety of nations. On the contrary, all efforts were marshalled at trying to confirm the composer's German-ness and strong identification with the German nation. Musicologists scoured out all surviving documentary material to support this interpretation. A letter written in May 1785 – in which Mozart railed against the overbearing influence of mediocre Italian opera composers in Vienna, and protested his right to read, speak and sing in German – provided them with the necessary ammunition. This outburst would be cited on numerous occasions as the clinching evidence that the composer was a true and patriotic German.

Rewriting the script

Taking isolated statements out of context may have enabled the Nazis to support the notion of Mozart's strong national consciousness. On the other hand, it was far more difficult to construct a similar case for his music. Undeterred by this problem, writers nonetheless made strenuous efforts to present a racial gloss on Mozart's operas. Ignoring the potent Italian influence in his music, they brandished *Die Entführung aus dem Serail* (The abduction from the Seraglio) as the first German national opera – a work in which Mozart engaged in furious battle with the 'mediocre' Italians, managing in the process to supplant their negative influence on late 18th-century Vienna's musical life. That the composer's subsequent operas were set in Italian was of little relevance. Anyone could perceive the sense of dignity and nobility in *The Marriage of Figaro* and the exploration of the darker side of human passion in *Don Giovanni* to be fundamentally German characteristics. Furthermore, in his final opera *Die Zauberflöte* (The Magic Flute), Mozart returned to his own language, demonstrating, in the words of Propaganda Minister Joseph Goebbels, that his innate feeling for popular melody qualified him to

SPIN-DOCTOR: German Minister of Propaganda Joseph Goebbels stands alongside Adolf Hitler

be regarded as a 'national artist in the best sense of the word'.

It's no surprise then that such generalisations ignored certain problematic and uncomfortable aspects of Mozart's life. As long-standing opponents of Freemasonry, which they regarded in the same conspiratorial league as World Jewry, they were obviously desperate to suppress the unambiguous evidence that Mozart had been an enthusiastic Freemason and – even worse – that *The Magic Flute* was imbued with all kinds of Masonic symbolism. And if that weren't enough, Mozart's favourite librettist Lorenzo Da Ponte, who wrote the texts for *The Marriage of Figaro*, *Don Giovanni* and *Così fan tutte*, happened to be a baptised Jew! Since artistic collaboration between Aryan and Jew was effectively outlawed in the Third Reich, the operas could conceivably have been banned had they not been such cornerstones of the repertory. Given this huge inconvenience, the only thing to do was to downgrade Da Ponte's contribution to these works – a task that many writers

of the period undertook with relish. Da Ponte was attacked in articles, books and programme notes with all manner of anti-Semitic stereotypes as self-seeking, unscrupulous and money-grabbing. Furthermore, it was fair game to assume that his texts were poor – a weak link in the creative chain that Mozart's 'Aryan' genius had somehow managed to overcome. Absurd and unsubstantiated claims were made to suggest that Mozart, rather than Da Ponte, had composed the text in certain sections of the operas. In some extreme cases, Da Ponte's name was excised from programmes, as if to deny his existence.

One way that the Nazis could have circumvented the Da Ponte problem was to insist that the operas on which they collaborated could only be performed in German translation. In this way, the argument followed, the Jewish element would no longer be so perceptible, while a German text could only serve to reinforce Mozart's sense of national identity. All this might have worked out well had it not been for the long-standing popularity of the

ALAMY X2

HARD AT WORK: Many top musicians took part in Mozart's anniversary year, including Richard Strauss

translations made at the end of the 19th century by Hermann Levi – a conductor of Jewish descent – which still featured in most German opera houses. But the fact that Levi's translations prevailed was eventually turned to the advantage of the Nazi regime. The climate of virulent anti-Semitism encouraged all manner of opportunists to try their hand at creating viable alternatives to Levi, and gain credit for 'rescuing' Mozart from the clutches of a sinister Jewish cabal.

Although opera houses were pretty well disposed towards singing Mozart in German, many singers were understandably reluctant to spend extra time learning new translations and resisted the imposition of Aryan alternatives to Hermann Levi. But given the necessity to drive out every particle of Jewish influence on German musical life, they could only hold out for a limited period of time. Yet although various 'Aryan' translations were assiduously promoted during the mid-1930s, Joseph Goebbels was surprisingly reluctant to rule in favour of one version. This only

Absurd and unsubstantiated claims were made to suggest that Mozart, rather than Da Ponte, had composed the text

changed with the establishment of a State Commission for the Re-arrangement of Music in 1939. One of its first actions was to commission new translations of all three of Mozart's Da Ponte operas by the musicologist Georg Schünemann. Published with the personal imprimatur of Goebbels, these translations were to be adopted by all opera houses on the orders of the Nazi regime. Somewhat astonishingly, these versions are still in print today.

Amadeus by order
With everything in place, it was now possible to make the greatest political capital out of the Mozart anniversary year. Almost all the major German cities held special Mozart Festivals, carefully

timed so as not to coincide with each other. A whole stream of books on Mozart appeared at the same time, some with titles that emphasised the composer's German heritage. Radio also got in on the act, with an ambitious set of 14 extended programmes from September to December 1941, which traced a chronological course through the various stages in Mozart's life. High-profile conductors Richard Strauss, Wilhelm Furtwängler, Karl Böhm, Clemens Krauss and Hans Knappertsbusch were on board, and the authorities were keen to make as large a topical point as possible. To achieve this, they enabled individual programmes to be broadcast from studios in key cities throughout Europe that Mozart had visited and were now occupied ▶

ENCORE: Wilhelm Furtwängler conducts the orchestra for Hitler and his associates

by the German army. Conceivably, the Germans might have hoped that one of the programmes in the schedule could have been beamed from London, which hosted Mozart's earliest appearances as a child. However, for obvious reasons, this plan never materialised.

As much of Germany was in the grip of Mozart fever, you would expect the two cities of Salzburg and Vienna, where the composer lived and worked, to have embraced the sanctification of Mozart most fervently. Particular significance was attached to the Salzburg Festival in the summer of 1941. One of the principal aims of the event was to provide members of the Wehrmacht with the opportunity for rest and instruction. On the orders of the regime, the streets of Mozart's birthplace thronged with an estimated 20,000 people in military uniforms, and Goebbels himself placed a memorial wreath in the room where the composer had been born.

The extraordinary festivities that took place in Vienna between November and December 1941, however, eclipsed Salzburg's homage to its most famous musician. In fact two festivals were

mounted simultaneously in the Austrian capital. The one organised by the city of Vienna was intended to reflect local and civic pride at Mozart's achievement. While the festival featured the usual series of orchestral concerts and operas, the prime intention seems to have been to involve Vienna's younger citizens in the deification of Mozart. To inculcate youth

Much of Germany was in the grip of Mozart fever

in this manner, every single primary and secondary school in Vienna's 26 districts was expected to hold its own special Mozart celebration, and the Hitler Youth also chipped in with ceremonies.

But the local festival inevitably played second fiddle to the Mozartwoche des Deutschen Reiches (Mozart Week of the German Reich), which took place in Vienna between 28 November and 5 December

and was organised under the auspices of the Propaganda Ministry in Berlin. The regime appeared to spare no effort or expense in bringing together a galaxy of star singers, instrumentalists and conductors who effectively made up the majority of the most famous musicians working in Germany at that time. Each day featured at least three or four different musical events including such luminaries as the pianists Edwin Fischer and Wilhelm Backhaus, and culminated in an evening performance of one of Mozart's six mature operas. *Die Entführung* opened proceedings with the conductor Karl Böhm and the cast of the Vienna State Opera. The following day the Munich Opera under Clemens Krauss performed *Così fan tutte*. The Vienna State Opera then returned for a seemingly punishing schedule of four different operas, *Don Giovanni* and *The Magic Flute* conducted by Hans Knappertsbusch, Karl Böhm taking the reins for *The Marriage of Figaro* and the veteran Richard Strauss performing the then rarely-heard *Idomeneo* in his own arrangement. Germany's greatest conductor Wilhelm Furtwängler arrived

ALAMY X2, GETTY

THE FINALE: The Musikverein in Vienna where Mozart's Requiem was the last performance during Mozartwoche in 1941

Mozartwoche – some of the major participants

Wilhelm Backhaus (1884-1969)
The favourite German pianist of the Führer, now best remembered for his intellectual performances of Beethoven and Brahms.

Clemens Krauss (1893-1954)
Austrian conductor, who took the reins for *Cosi fan tutte*. Appointed general artistic director of the Salzburg Festival the following year.

Hans Knappertsbusch (1888-1965)
Great German conductor, who conducted *Don Giovanni* and *Die Zauberflöte*. Today, is more favourably remembered for his outstanding Wagner performances.

Karl Böhm (1894-1981)
An Austrian conductor who managed to play down his Nazi affiliations in the post-war era. Conducted *Die Entführung aus dem Serail* and *The Marriage of Figaro*.

Wilhelm Furtwängler (1886-1954)
The greatest interpreter of the core German repertory in the 20th century – unlike others, refused to join the Nazi party. Conducted Mozart's Requiem.

Richard Strauss (1864-1949)
The composer and conductor idolised Mozart and, in 1931, made a highly regarded arrangement of his opera *Idomeneo*, which he conducted at the Mozartwoche.

Edwin Fischer (1886-1960)
A Swiss pianist who was living in Germany. He is now regarded as one of the greatest players of the 20th century, and an eminent instructor of the piano.

in Vienna on the final day, which marked the actual anniversary of the composer's death, to conduct a moving performance of Mozart's Requiem in the Musikverein.

Amadeus by order

The Nazi political hierarchy seized the opportunity to declare its unbridled enthusiasm for Mozart, while making sure that everyone understood the topical relevance of the celebrations. At the opening concert on 28 November 1941, the Reichsleiter of Vienna and former leader of the Hitler Youth, Baldur von Schirach, delivered a lengthy speech in which he underlined the festival's significance and tried to contrast what he perceived to be the 'cultural sterility' of Great Britain and the United States with the idealistic aspirations of the German nation. It was at this juncture that von Schirach made the notorious claim that those fighting for Germany, were also fighting in the name of Mozart.

In what must have been a thinly concealed veneer of political in-fighting, Propaganda Minister Joseph Goebbels came to Vienna a week later, making sure that his own speech on Mozart, delivered before an enthusiastic audience that had assembled to hear a concert by the Vienna Philharmonic in the State Opera House, would have even more impact than that of his rival von Schirach. Underlining the idea that Mozart's music was among the most precious things that the German soldier was defending, the ultimate master of spin saw no contradiction between the world of sound in which Mozart lived and worked and 'the hard and threatening world we are experiencing, the chaos of which we want to transform into discipline and order.'

On the following day, just before Furtwängler's performance of the Requiem, Mozart was canonized at a special rally held in front of St. Stephan's cathedral. The party leadership unveiled a newly constructed Mozart monument with a burning memorial flame. Baldur von Schirach delivered the Hitler salute and lay olive wreathes from the Führer, Goering and von Ribbentrop in Mozart's honour. Then representatives from 18 of Germany's allies and members of the public gathered to pay their respects, while the sound of bells from all Vienna's churches resounded in praise of the immortal composer. ■

LEADING THE MUSIC: Hans Knappertsbusch conducted two operas during the festival

MOZART

THE MAGIC FLUTE

Seebuehne theatre, Austria, 2013. Dir. David Pountney

Mozart's *Singspiel The Magic Flute* **promises audiences deceit, love, suspense and plenty of masonic references.**

PA IMAGES

Masonry and The Magic Flute

A keen Freemason, Mozart riddled
Die Zauberflöte with references to the fraternity.
HC Robbins Landon explains the hidden agenda

O n 14 December 1784, Mozart joined the Order of Freemasons, that 'Ancient and Honourable Institution', which was, and still is, based on values of integrity, honesty, kindness and fairness. Mozart's lodge was the small Viennese 'Zur Wohltätigkeit', which often operated within the much larger and grander lodge, 'Zur wahren Eintracht', where his musical friend Joseph Haydn was also soon to become a member. As with all Masons, Mozart joined as an 'Entered Apprentice', the first of three degrees – the second stage is entitled 'Fellow Craft' and the third 'Master Mason'. Mozart became a devoted Freemason, and he rose through the ranks quickly; to the second degree on 7 January 1785 and the third shortly after. His commitment to the brotherhood shows through in his music; as well as

> ## THE BELIEFS OF THE ORDER CAN BE FOUND IN MANY OF MOZART'S LATER PIECES

writing several pieces especially for Masonic gatherings, the beliefs and symbols of the order can be found in many of his later pieces for public performance, too. But, arguably, none are more overt than *The Magic Flute*, for which he collaborated with fellow Freemason and librettist, Emanuel Schikaneder.

A story to tell

The Masonic message of the time was parallel to that of the Enlightenment, rather than the ritual or the occult, with which it may be more commonly associated these days. The brotherhood vehemently believed that darkness would disappear before light, goodness would conquer all evil and that courage was more than cowardice. One doesn't have to look hard to find these themes prevalent in the plot of *The Magic Flute*.

ALAMY

LEADING LADY: The Queen of the Night was first performed by Mozart's sister-in-law Josepha Weber

SECRET SOCIETY: Zur Wohltätigkeit, the Freemason's lodge that Mozart joined in 1784

While the opera's subject is not original – German scholars have carefully traced its precursors – Schikaneder's word book for *The Magic Flute* contains a whole series of archetypal figures with which the public can instantly recognise. Good and bad are carefully balanced between the 'evil' Queen of the Night and the virtuous priests, while simple folk-like characters such as Papageno (played by Schikaneder himself at the premiere) and Papagena, his bride, are countered with the noble Prince Tamino and Princess Pamina. There is more than just an excellent balancing act going on here, though. Schikaneder has drawn out the beliefs of the Masons, weaving them into the plot. He even includes some daringly undisguised elements to make his point: during the final chorus, the words 'Es siegte die Stärke und kroner zum Lohn/die Schönheit und Weisheit mit ewiger Kron' ('Strength conquers and crowns with its rewards/ beauty and wisdom with an eternal crown') are sung out. As well as

> **'IF A MASTER MASON YOU WOULD BE, OBSERVE YOU WELL THE RULE OF THREE...' THE MASON'S EXAMINATION, 1723**

perfectly articulating the message of Enlightenment, this is taken almost word-for-word from an ancient Masonic ritual.

Powerful friends

Schikaneder wasn't the only Freemason to behave less-than covertly – during the late 18th century, the brotherhood thrived in Austria. An author of the time, Caroline Pichler, whose father was a prominent Mason, relates in her memoirs that, 'The order of Freemasons carried on its activities with an almost absurd publicity. Freemason songs were printed, composed and sung everywhere.' She goes on to explain the many benefits of membership: 'It was not unadvantageous to belong to this brotherhood, which had members in every circle and had the know-how to entice leaders, presidents and governors into its bosom. For there, one brother helped the other...and during the last

REX FEATURES

years of the reign of Joseph II, they caused a great deal of mischief.' Indeed, they caused so much mischief that Emperor Joseph II severely curtailed the brotherhood's activities in the 1780s, and the Craft would be banned in 1795, after conspiracies emerged that Austrian Masons were involved in an attempt to overthrow the government. Masonry remained banned in Austria until 1918.

As a result of the fusions required by the Emperor in 1785, Mozart entered into a new lodge, called 'Crowned Hope' (later 'New Crowned Hope'). In 1790, that lodge's Master of Ceremonies was none other than Prince Nikolaus Esterházy – Haydn's noble patron. So when Schikaneder presented Mozart with the word book for *The Magic Flute*, which was filled with Masonic symbols, the composer was eager to set them to music – after all, it would be sure to impress his Master of Ceremonies, his new lodge, and all the Brothers in Vienna.

It's a magic number

Freemasons used many symbols to make themselves known to their brothers, and to communicate in confidence. Their symbols are part of the Craft's secret ritualism, but some are not-so secret

anymore. A booklet was printed in London in 1725, entitled *The Grand Mystery of the Free Masons Discovered*, and although quite a mysterious publication in itself – the original was supposedly found on the body of a Mason who had passed away – it seems to reveal some of the important symbols of Freemasonry. In the *Examination Upon Entrance into the Lodge* one learns that the number three is of great significance. There are three 'precious Jewels' – a 'square Asher [Ashet, ie, dish or platter], a Diamond and a Square' – three lights, three steps to becoming a mason, three 'particular Points [that] pertain to a Free Mason', namely 'Fraternity, Fidelity and Taciturnity' and in 1723, another print entitled *The Mason's Examination* revealed: 'If a Master Mason you would be, Observe you well the Rule of Three...'

It is no surprise therefore, that many a trinity is artfully littered throughout *The Magic Flute*. To name a few, there are three flats in the key signature of E flat, three main male and female roles, three child spirits – represented with frail and beautiful melodies – three trombones and, in the Overture and later when the music returns, the famous 'three chords', symbolic of the Masonic knock, which opens and closes a Masonic lodge. In multiples of three, we ▶

FIRE AND WATER:
Two of the ordeals that
Tamino has to go through

find that there are 18 priests, and that Sarastro, the High Priest, first appears in Act I, Scene 18. Completing the symbolism further, the priests' majestic ritual music brings forth visions of the grand rites and ceremonies performed by Master Masons in their lodges.

The Magic Flute abounds in other Masonic symbols, too – in the music as much as in the action. During the middle of the Overture, the music stops and the rhythmic sign for the second degree of Freemasonry, that of the Fellow Craft, is presented in the winds and the brass. The reason for this is that Tamino, the Prince, has yet to undergo his final ritual and become, symbolically, a Master Mason – the third degree. And Tamino's trials offer other fraternal connections. His first tests are to remain silent – resonant of each Mason's responsibility to keep the secrets of the order. And the final trials are to test his fear of death and encourage bravery – exactly the same quality that is tested in Masonry initiates.

Behind every great man...

There is one extraordinary point about the Masonic content of the opera, which must be stressed. When the time comes for Tamino's initiation, to which we have referred above, he is not alone. In a normal Masonic lodge, the Masons enter two by two (but in the rite of initiation the Mason is alone, of course). Tamino, however, enters not with another man but with his lady, Pamina.

Women had no role in Freemasonry, except in France where female lodges still exist today. Sarastro, the worshipful master in *The Magic Flute*, is distinctly anti-feminist. So what is Pamina doing in this crucial scene? This is a purely Mozartian concept. In all his mature operas, women play a vital role, and Mozart was the first

> ## IT IS CLEAR THAT MOZART'S PASSION FOR FREEMASONRY WAS HUGELY INFLUENTIAL AT THE TIME OF WRITING

operatic composer to investigate the hopes, loves and tragedies of the fairer sex, to interpret lovingly their motivations and reactions. In all his stage works of his last decade, loving forgiveness from females plays a central part. Here, in *The Magic Flute*, did Mozart hope to reform the Masonry to which he belonged by asking that women be included in the Craft's membership?

Much more than Masonry

Ultimately, one may never know exactly what Mozart hoped to achieve through his representation of the Craft in *The Magic Flute*. However, when one studies the symbols, the plot and the references in the music, it is clear that his passion for Freemasonry was hugely influential at the time of writing. Indeed, there is something infinitely touching about this great Mozartian tribute. But it would be doing the composer an injustice to suggest that this *Singspiel* is merely a platform through which to preach the Masonic morals. What Mozart actually created is one of the great touchstones of opera – calling on sublime music, identifiable characters and a finely honed plot – all built around the philosophical ideals of Freemasonry, set at its heart. ∎

THE POWER OF THREE:
Three is symbolic to
Freemasons, hence Mozart's
three ladies in the opera

Remembering Mozart

After Mozart's death, Europe paid its respects in abundance, but it wouldn't be long until his music fell out of fashion, as Neal Zaslaw explains

W hen Mozart died on 5 December 1791, his music was known and loved across Europe, and in the New World as well. Word of his death spread and an outpouring of tributes began, in the visual arts, prose, poetry and music. Composer Anton Eberl was

quick off the mark, writing a cantata, *At Mozart's Grave*, which was completed in Vienna only six days after Mozart's death. Eberl certainly knew Mozart and may have received instruction from him. A few years later he toured with Constanze Mozart, her sons and her sister, giving concerts for the children's benefit. An assistant music director in Berlin, Carl Bernhard Wessely was almost as fast as Eberl, and by the end of December had set a poem by Gottlob Wilhelm Burmann, *Mozart's Urn*, which was published the following year. Tombstones and funerary urns were popular on the title pages of Mozart memorials – understandable, given that knowledge of his unmarked grave was not yet widespread.

Mourning in Scandinavia

When news of Mozart's demise reached Stockholm three weeks after the event, Sweden's troubadour, Carl Michael Bellman, wrote a poem, *Öfver Mozart's död* (Mozart's death). Joseph Martin Kraus, who had known Mozart in Vienna in 1783, set it to music, and they performed it for friends on 5 January 1792. For whatever reasons, ▶

QUICK OFF THE MARK:
Anton Eberl was the first to write a memorial piece

ALAMY X2

A FAMILY AFFAIR:
Franz Xaver conducted
a medley of his
father's work in 1842

LASTING LEGACY:
Unlike other pieces, Mozart's Requiem
remained popular throughout the 19th century

Bellman and Kraus hung onto this touching song, not allowing it to be published.

Masonic music

Another cantata, with anonymous text 'to be sung on the one-year anniversary of Mozart's death', composed by Franz Danzi, was duly ready for its Munich premiere on 5 December 1792. For Mozart's fellow Masons, Karl Friedrich Hensler wrote an oration and poem, which were delivered early in 1792 at The Most Worthy Lodge of St John, called *The Crowned Hope in the Orient*. The opening lines convey the flavour:

Rise! Mourn for him as Masons,
Whom Fate for Brother gave;
Too soon from us he hastens,
Down to a somber grave.
With gentleness and patience,
A Mason heart and soul,
He lifts our aspirations
Toward a higher goal.
The bond is snapped!
We give him

Our blessings and our love;
Our brother-love shall guide him
To harmony above.

England too mourned, with the assistance of composer Samuel Webbe, who translated from the German and adjusted the music to an otherwise unknown vocal quartet 'from the Epicedium on Mozart'. From Prague, so in love with Mozart and he with it, came a number of tributes, including this one by Joseph Georg Meinerth, used to introduce a memorial concert of the composer's music:

He was too early taken from our midst
Who touched the chords of feeling with
such skill,
And brought their sharpest tones in
harmony.
An angry thunder-breathing God has
struck
Where flowed before the peaceful
meadow springs.
And now the strings' vibrations and
the songs

Of rapture, and the turmoil of the heart
All help to bring to mind the sleeping life
Attend! Angelic harmonies ring out
'Tis Mozart! Crowned he is with radiance,
And in your very midst his spirit moves
On fairy footsteps.

Even if this appears sentimental, kitschy and even maudlin to our modern perceptions, I don't doubt its sincerity. After all, more than two centuries on, many of us have seen music-lovers visibly moved contemplating Mozart's early demise. Tributes continued, only slightly less intensively, until 1856. Mozart's 100th birthday fuelled a final frenzy of publications, speeches, statues, memorial tablets and the like. In Salzburg, the still-standing statue of Mozart had been dedicated in 1842. His youngest son, Franz Xaver, with the older son, Carl, in attendance, conducted a cantata (*Festival Chorus for the Unveiling Ceremony of the Mozart Monument in Salzburg*) for which he wrote new words fitted to a medley of his father's most famous works. Constanze

PERIOD COSTUME:
The Mozart Festival Orchestra bring
Mozart to a 21st-century audience

Mozart, who worked tirelessly to make this happen, had died only a few months earlier.

Changing tastes

Alongside the tributes, however, the status of Mozart's music began to change. In the early half of the 19th century, large amounts of it were readily available in print. People played and sang his music at home and taught it to their children. Yet beloved and admired as Mozart's music remained, the programmes for public concerts and operas reveal that progressively less of it was being performed publicly. After a burst of popularity early in the century, *La clemenza di Tito* mostly vanished. Of the Da Ponte trilogy, *Figaro* and *Don Giovanni* were performed (often in bowdlerised versions), and *The Magic Flute* was ever popular. The ambiguous *Così fan tutte* was largely avoided, or rewritten to change the story. Among the orchestral works, only a handful of the concertos and symphonies were heard. The emphasis had shifted to works in minor keys and works that could bear the

> MORE THAN TWO CENTURIES ON, MANY OF US HAVE SEEN MUSIC-LOVERS VISIBLY MOVED CONTEMPLATING MOZART'S EARLY DEMISE

enlarged spaces and enlarged orchestras of the Romantic era (the Requiem, for example). Anything light or delicate, meant to be heard close-up, suffered. He and his music began to seem too much implicated in the *ancient regime*, too light, too old-fashioned, too much smelling of powdered wigs. Mozart had been demoted to the status of 'forerunner.'

A new audience

A revival began towards the end of the century, when Saint-Saëns and others started to champion the piano concertos, Mahler *et al* rediscovered the operas in their original form, and a generation of younger conductors awoke the symphonies and overtures. In Catholic Austria, even

after generations of attempted liturgical reform and opposition from the Caecilian movement, Mozart's masses and other sacred works were performed for their original functions. And then the 20th century arrived... Stravinsky and other composers, seeking ways out of the Wagnerisation of their craft were desperate to create neo-Baroque and neo-Classical styles. The 'chamber orchestra' was an early 20th century phenomenon. Mozart was fashionable again. And since then, allowing for a certain ebb and flow, he remains ensconced as the composer who seems easy to play but isn't, easy to sing but isn't and easy to understand, but isn't. He is a perpetual icon and crowd-pleaser. Just as he always was. ■

A wandering minstrel

It is tempting to see Mozart as a product of musical history, an heir to the legacies of JS Bach and Handel, and a student, in a way, of his contemporary, Haydn. But Cliff Eisen argues that he was not – not really

Mozart's 18th century was not so concerned with music history – at least not the way we are – and musical styles were influenced largely by the works of the composers around at the time, though by no means all of them. During the mid-18th century, there was far less international or transcultural circulation of music than now, and cultural and social differences, religion and tastes often prevented performances of any particular repertory at any particular court, theatre or other public venue. So Mozart 'arose' not out of some grand music-historical process but out of his exposure to specific music at different times and places, and the opportunities to compose offered to him by his appointment at Salzburg, his freelance years in Vienna, and his many travels. His legacy may have been historical, but his origins were immediate and of his own time and place.

The European effect
At Salzburg, where Mozart was chiefly based until early 1781, he studied the church music of the court composer Ernst Eberlin, his father Leopold, and his older colleagues Anton Cajetan Adlgasser and Michael Haydn; from these he learned not only traditional Fuxian counterpoint but also some aspects of contemporaneous Italian church music, including the modern vocal forms often found in these works. His church music of the time reflects both these influences. In London in 1764-65, he had his first sustained exposure to Italianate symphonies, chiefly through the works of Johann Christian Bach, and Italian opera. These lessons were put into practice in his earliest symphonies (K16, 19, 19a and 22, all written between 1764 and 1766) and during his three trips to Italy between 1769 and 1773, in *Mitridate*, *Il sogno di Scipione* and *Lucio Silla*. When he visited Vienna in 1773, Mozart absorbed local chamber music styles, chiefly string quartets by Gassmann and Haydn, and composed his own, K168. The florid Mannheim style figures prominently in the piano sonata K309, written when the composer visited the German city in 1777. Conspicuously absent from this account is French music, which Mozart heard during his visits to Paris in 1764, 1766 and 1778.

And it is absent because in Mozart's view, 'the whole of French music isn't worth a tinker's curse' (letter from 1 February 1764). It's not just that French music did not appeal to the Mozarts – French culture on the whole was foreign, strange and unappealing, and the cultural politics of Paris opaque and difficult to negotiate.

What Mozart did learn in Paris came from the works of expatriate German composers living there. Leontzi Honauer, Johann Gottfried Eckard, Johann Schobert and Hermann Friedrich Raupach all gave Mozart copies of their printed works, which he later arranged, together with movements from Carl Philipp and Emanuel Bach, as the Concertos K37 and K39-41.

The influence of others
If music history does play a role in Mozart's development, it's primarily during his Viennese decade from 1781 to 1791. For, although he had encountered some of Handel's music during his

> HIS LEGACY MAY HAVE BEEN HISTORICAL, BUT HIS ORIGINS WERE OF HIS OWN TIME AND PLACE

GETTY

VIENNESE SCHOOL: Mozart was a product of his upbringing, influenced by many of the local music styles he encountered

visit to London in 1764-65, he was mostly unfamiliar with the great oratorios until the late 1780s, when he was commissioned to arrange them for private performance. And he possibly did not know any of Bach's works before his move to Vienna, where he made string quartet arrangements of selections from the Well Tempered Clavier for the private music gatherings organised by Gottfried van Swieten. There was no call for these kinds of works in Salzburg, neither that of the 'English' Handel nor the German, Lutheran Bach.

An amalgamation of styles

But the lessons he learned in Vienna from both composers profoundly affected his style. The elegant contrapuntal thinking of many of his instrumental works owes much to Bach, even if he rarely adopts a Baroque style. When he does, it is conspicuous and deliberate, as in the chorus of the armed men in *The Magic Flute*, possibly a direct result of his encounter with Bach's motet 'Singer dem Herrn' in Leipzig in 1789. And the Requiem is in many respects unthinkable without the model of Handel, from whom Mozart learnt much about the relationship between musicians. It was this universality, and this awareness of the 'localness' of musical culture, that allowed Mozart to succeed in Vienna, which in many respects offered the best of all possible musical worlds for him as both composer and performer. The Viennese upper classes and nobility provided him with pupils, opportunities to perform privately, and public support for his subscription concerts. The court sponsored both German and Italian opera and appointed Mozart as Kammermusicus in 1787. Even the church, though limited by Emperor Joseph II's Enlightenment reforms, nevertheless supported Mozart by engaging him as music director at St Stephen's Cathedral (though he died before he could take up the

post). In addition, music publishers actively printed and promoted his music. Mozart's musical origins were of his own time and place, from whence he took both some characteristic thematic material as well as his thinking about the relationship among soloists, chorus and fugue.

Globalisation and Mozart

It was in Vienna, too, that Mozart first became acquainted with a substantial number of Haydn's works, and in response to which he composed, among other works, six quartets dedicated to the older master (K387, K421, K428, K458, K464 and K465). As Mozart wrote in his dedication: 'May it...please you to receive them kindly and to be their father, guide and friend!' Paradoxically perhaps, it was the fragmentation of contemporaneous musical culture that may have contributed most to Mozart's universality. For unlike virtually all other composers of the time, he had the chance to experience these different musical cultures mostly first-hand.

Together with a rise in music journalism, increasing numbers of public concerts and improvements in travel, the globalisation of music in the late 1780s and 1790s played no small part in the spread of Mozart's reputation. Towards the end of his life, his works were available, written about and performed not only in German-speaking Europe but also England, France, Italy and as far afield as Russia and the US. It was this globalisation that also catapulted Haydn and Beethoven to universal fame, and before long, history had invented a triumvirate of 'classical' Viennese composers that was to dominate musical thinking for much of the next century.

In the end, Mozart may have been a product of culture, but he was not a product of history – on the contrary, together with Haydn and Beethoven, Mozart in a sense 'created' musical history. ■

Mozart's cities

Which cities had the greatest effect on the young genius as he made his way around Europe? Chris de Souza gets his atlas out

tarting with his grand tour of Europe in 1763, Mozart travelled extensively, finding fame wherever he went. As a child, he enjoyed success all over Europe before moving to Vienna in his twenties to live out the last decade of his life.

Salzburg

Born in Salzburg, many of the buildings in which Mozart lived and worked still stand. One gets a sense of how the work of the court and church shaped his first musical experiences, and of the provinciality that would drive him away.

London

The Mozarts spent from April 1764 to July 1765 in London. They stayed first in Frith (then, ironically, Thrift) Street. The Hanover Square concert rooms were not far, nor the Brook-Street home of the then recently deceased Handel, whose music Mozart heard for the first time. He met JC Bach, a greater influence on Mozart's mature style than any other composer.

His first symphonies (written in Ebury St) were performed, and he saw Bach's *Adriano in Siria* at the King's (now Her Majesty's) Theatre in Haymarket.

Milan

At 14, Mozart's opera *Mitridate* was premiered and after its success, *Ascanio in Alba* was commissioned for the wedding of Archduke Ferdinand and Beatrice d'Este. For it, Giovanni Manzuoli, who gave Mozart his first singing lessons in London, came out of retirement to create the title role. *Lucio Silla* was premiered there in December 1772 – his work over the Christmas period was possibly fuelled by panettone!

Paris

As a youngster he had been received by royalty – the Mozarts attended the King at dinner in Versailles and they stayed in the Rue Francois-Miron. In 1778 he went again, staying near Montmartre, but this time suffered a series of humiliations – and also his mother's death. Mozart wrote 'On foot it is too far everywhere – or too muddy, for the filth in Paris is not to be described', but musically he learned much from the style of French opera and ballet, and the French fashion for Sinfonia concertantes.

Prague

At the Estates Theatre, where he conducted *Figaro* and the premiere of *Don Giovanni* in 1787, performances of the latter are still given regularly. Mozart felt appreciated by the Bohemians and spent a happy time with his friends, the Duseks, at their villa. He was in Prague again in the last year of his life for the premiere of *La clemenza di Tito*. It is a handy point of departure for a trip to Brno, which is also proud of its Mozart connections.

Vienna

Mozart's home for the last dozen years of his life is a very different city now. The Figarohaus, where Mozart lived, just behind the cathedral, is a sadly empty experience. ■

Sweet sounds
Gavin Dixon unwraps the story behind Salzburg's Mozart balls

If ever you are deciding on presents to bring back from a holiday in Salzburg, chances are your thoughts will turn to Mozart balls. Mozartkugeln, to give them their less innuendo-prone German name, have been handmade by the Fürst family for 120 years. When Paul Fürst introduced his 'Mozartbonbon' in 1890 it was an innovation on two counts, not only the first chocolate to be named after a famous composer but also, and perhaps more impressively, the first to be perfectly spherical with no flat surfaces. The recipe is simple but effective: a pistachio marzipan centre wrapped in nougat and, finally, dipped in dark chocolate.

Fürst's expertise in confectionery turned out to be in advance of his business skills, and when his Mozartkugeln became popular, competitors soon discovered that he had not patented the recipe. As a result, most Mozart balls on the market today are by other makers and most are mass-produced. It is easy to spot the real thing though, as only the original Fürst product can be called 'Salzburg Mozartkugeln'. As a rule, any Mozart ball with the word 'real' (*echt*) in the name is an imitation. But whether original or just 'real', Salzburg takes great pride in its Mozart-themed confectionery. Oversized Mozartkugeln are a common sight in shop windows around the city. In 2006, the council took the idea further and installed 80 giant polyester replicas around the old town. The project made the headlines but for the wrong reasons, when vandals unbolted one of the balls and rolled it round the streets causing damage estimated at €7,000 (£5,900). Mozartkugeln, however, aren't to everybody's taste, so the Fürsts offer some other choices. Why not try a square chocolate filled with coffee and nut truffle? It has a memorable name, although you might see a pattern emerging – they're called Bachwurfel or Bach Cubes.

BBC MUSIC MAGAZINE SUBSCRIPTION ORDER FORM

Complete the order form and send to *BBC Music Magazine*,
FREEPOST, LON16059, Sittingbourne, Kent ME9 8DF

☑ **YES, I would like to subscribe to *BBC Music Magazine***

DIRECT DEBIT PAYMENT OPTION

☐ **UK Direct Debit – 5 issues for £5**   **BEST BUY**
   (Please complete the Direct Debit mandate below)

Instructions to your Bank or Building Society to pay by Direct Debit   DIRECT Debit

TO: The Manager (Bank/Building Society)

Address

Postcode

Name(s) of Account Holder(s)

Bank/Building Society account number   **Branch sort code**

Reference Number (Internal use only)

Originator's identification number

7 1 0 6 4 4

Please pay Immediate Media Co Bristol Ltd Debits from the account detailed in this instruction subject to the safeguards assured by the Direct Debit Guarantee. I understand that this instruction may remain with Immediate Media Co Bristol Ltd and, if so, details will be passed electronically to my Bank/Building Society.

Signature   Date   /   /

Banks and Building Societies may not accept Direct Debit Instructions from some types of account.

YOUR DETAILS (Essential)   MOZP13

Title   First name   Surname

Address

Town   Postcode

Home telephone number

Mobile telephone number††

Email address††

Immediate Media Company Limited (Publishers of *BBC Music Magazine*) would love to keep you informed by post or telephone of special offers and promotions from the Immediate Media Company Group. Please tick if you'd prefer not to receive these ☐.

†† Please enter this information so that *BBC Music Magazine* may keep you informed of newsletters, special offers and other promotions by email or text message. You may unsubscribe from these at any time. Please tick here if you'd like to receive details of special offers from BBC Worldwide via email ☐.

GIVE A GIFT SUBSCRIPTION – If you would like to give a subscription to *BBC Music Magazine* to a friend, tick this box ■ and include the recipient's address details on a separate sheet.

OTHER PAYMENT METHODS For a year's subscription (13 issues)

☐ **UK cheque/credit card** – £48.60 for 13 issues   **SAVE 25%***
☐ **Europe** £65.00 for 13 issues
☐ **Rest of World** £74.00 for 13 issues
   USA $99/**Canada** $131.40 – Please call toll free 1-800 342 3592
   South African subscribers call +27 011 265 4303
☐ I enclose a cheque made payable to *Immediate Media Co Bristol Ltd* for £ _____

Overseas subscribers post form to: BBC Music Magazine, PO Box 279, Sittingbourne, Kent ME9 8DF, UK

CREDIT CARD   ☐ Visa ☐ Mastercard ☐ Maestro

Card number

Valid from ☐☐/☐☐   Expiry date ☐☐/☐☐   Issue no ☐☐ (Maestro only)

Signature   Date

*5 issues for £5 offer available to UK residents paying by Direct Debit. After your trial period your payments will continue at £19.45 every 6 issues, saving 35% on the shop price. If you cancel within 2 weeks of receiving your 4th issue you will pay no more than £5. Your subscription will start with the next available issue.

OFFER ENDS 25 SEPTEMBER 2014

YOUR SPECIAL OFFER:

- **Pay just £5 for your first 5 issues**
- After your trial period, **continue to save 35%** on the shop price
- Benefit from **FREE UK home delivery** direct to your door
- Build up a listening library with a **complete work** on each month's cover CD
- **Never miss a single issue** of the world's best-selling classical music magazine!

Don't miss this fantastic offer
SUBSCRIBE TODAY

10 Mozart myths

Think that Mozart makes you clever, or that Salieri poisoned his 'rival'? Rob Ainsley invites you to think again

1. He was buried in a pauper's grave

Mozart was buried in an unmarked, 'simple' grave (not communal pit) standard then for Vienna's middle class. The poor were buried in sacks; Mozart probably wore a black suit, in a coffin bought by Constanze and Gottfried van Swieten.

2. He had Tourette's syndrome

In 1992, the British Medical Journal claimed that Mozart's mannerisms and his scatological letters showed he had Tourette's. But his bums-and-poo humour was evidence of high spirits and was common in middle-class Vienna.

3. He died rehearsing the Requiem

In the decades after his death, the new Romantic ideas of composer-as-tortured artist embroidered the story of the Requiem's composition. But the day-of-death rehearsal with friends, and his sobbing during the Lacrimosa, is fanciful: the last sing-through happened earlier.

4. Salieri poisoned him

As early as December 1791, the rumour was circulating, Pushkin wrote a play about it, and as late as 1984, the film *Amadeus* was based on the idea. But Constanze didn't think so, even though she said the dying, delirious Mozart mentioned it.

5. He wrote Symphonies Nos 39-41 as testament, for posterity

There's no firm evidence he heard them played. But he didn't write them for posterity: he was a pro, not an egotist. He undoubtedly wrote them for commercial performance, but was probably stymied by Vienna's 1788 recession.

6. As a teen he wrote out Allegri's Miserere after one hearing

Remembering and transcribing the layout of this formulaic piece was within his powers, but no Mozart manuscript is known. The only references are his father's vague letter at the time, and his sister's recollections 20 years later.

SOUNDS FICTIONAL: Mozart listening to Allegri's *Miserere*

7. He constructed a system for generating minuets by throwing dice

A portion of his String Quintet, K516f, manuscript has music fragments possibly associated with the alphabet – but no instructions on how to 'convert' names to melodies, and nothing about dice.

8. He wore brightly coloured wigs

Not only did Mozart never wear the party-joke hairpieces in *Amadeus* – he rarely wore a wig (only for official occasions). What you see in those portraits is his own fair hair, dressed and beribboned, as society men did then.

AWARD WINNING: Tom Hulce and Elizabeth Berridge star as Mozart and Constanze in the 1984 film *Amadeus*

9. Mozart increases your intelligence

Rauscher, Shaw and Ky (1993) reported that hearing ten minutes of Mozart's Sonata K448 temporarily increased IQ scores, compared to silence. But nobody else has replicated this – they've only concluded that it's an effect of mood.

10. A photograph of Constanze Mozart was taken in 1840

The old lady seen standing in a group photo at the house of composer Max Keller is almost certainly not Mozart's widow. In 1840, when the photo was supposedly taken, Constanze was crippled with arthritis and would not have been able to travel to see Keller. Furthermore, the lenses needed for such outdoor group shots were not pioneered until after her death in 1842. ■

TRUE OR FALSE: Could this be Mozart's wife?

THINKSTOCK, ALAMY, GETTY X2